DYLAN

BROTHERHOOD PROTECTORS WORLD

THE GUARDIAN AGENCY
BOOK ONE

REGAN BLACK

BROTHERHOOD PROTECTORS
ORIGINAL SERIES BY ELLE JAMES

ACKNOWLEDGMENTS

With special thanks to Elle James for inviting me into her world of Brotherhood Protectors

PROLOGUE

Two miles into his five mile route, Dylan Parker kept running when his cell phone chimed with a new alert. He'd anticipated at least a week of downtime after his previous assignment. Maybe this was a follow-up.

No such luck he realized as read the brief text message on his screen: Protect

It was the one-word signal that he was back on the clock. Two additional messages would arrive any second with a picture followed by the address and preliminary background file of the person whose life was now his responsibility.

He kept running, his shoes slapping against the ribbon of asphalt winding through the park, while he waited. When he saw the subject's address he calculated the travel time and took the next turn, cutting his run down to three miles.

Every minute counted for a client in danger.

CHAPTER 1

Austin, Texas
Wednesday, November 14, 3:55 p.m.

Jana Clayton turned onto North Congress Street, willing her wobbling knees to function properly as she walked into her father's favorite coffee shop. Given a choice, her appointment would've been held anywhere but here, on any day but today. Tucking her sunglasses into the buckle of her purse strap, she joined the line and hoped her waterproof mascara would hold up.

During the brief drive from home she'd blotted away fresh tears with each stoplight that gave her a clear view of the Texas capitol building. For the first time in her life, she cursed the city planners for their thoughtful and precise attention to that detail.

When she'd received confirmation of this meeting she had known maintaining her composure here would be one more personal challenge. Nearing the counter, she reminded herself that normal people didn't break down sobbing at the mention of a caramel macchiato or a shot of espresso.

Since her father had been found dead in his study almost two weeks ago she felt as far removed from normal as a person could get. In a heavy emotional fog, she'd slogged through countless 'final' decisions, and accepted a torrent of sympathy during the public and private memorial services. Instead of healing or easing the sting of grief, she felt worse with each passing day. It wasn't just the shock of losing the man who'd been her anchor and inspiration, it was the oppressive loneliness, the suffocating realization that the one person who understood her dreams and her heart would never see those dreams fulfilled.

Yes, it was all of that compounded by the letter from her father she'd mysteriously received just after the funeral. His last message to her scrawled by hand across the official Texas Senate stationery kept her in this perpetual state of turmoil. Today's meeting could change that, turn things around. She had to hang on to that hope.

Sniffling, she reached into the pocket of her short, forest green trench coat for a tissue to dab at her nose. She absolutely refused to take this meeting, one that could mean the difference between an honorable or a tarnished legacy for her father, with a nose Santa Claus could use on a cloudy night.

Reaching the counter, she straightened her spine and placed her order in a calm, steady voice.

The barista reached out and patted Jana's hand. "We're all so sorry about your dad, sweetie."

"Thank you." Jana managed a small smile.

"I nearly bawled my eyes out when I caught Sally Ann making the Senator's standing order this morning."

For years, this shop had provided coffee and pastries for the Wednesday staff meetings. Such happy routines had been irrevocably erased from Jana's weekly schedule. *Forever*. She nodded, feeling her polite smile slipping as she struggled for the right words. Her mascara didn't stand a chance if this kept up. It was important to listen, to let others share memories and express their grief, but every outpouring of sympathy felt like an emotional sucker punch, leaving her gasping for air. She was starting to believe her stepmother, Camille, had the right idea with her current tactic of hiding in a haze of valium behind the closed curtains and locked gates of the Clayton family ranch.

Oh, they all meant well, but with no one to help her carry the load, Jana felt herself cracking under the burden. Someone had to keep tabs on her father's political issues and business details. Someone had to be the public face of Senator Clayton's legacy of service. Based on the unpleasant and false rumors of depression revealed in this morning's paper, that someone was also going to have to put out a few fires along the way. Her personal agony could wait, it wasn't going anywhere, but she couldn't allow the press to steamroll her father's upstanding reputation.

"It will take us all some time to adjust," Jana said at last, taking her coffee. "He meant the world to so many people." Hopefully those people wouldn't believe the trashy gossip and speculation.

She stepped back from the counter, swiftly crossing to an open table near the wide front window. Her father had improved life for countless Texans. Despite his accomplishments during his thirty-year span as a senator, someone had killed him. Disguising it as suicide hadn't fooled her. She'd known it from the first phone call. As if hearing her father was dead hadn't been enough of a shock, bad had quickly turned worse when authorities labeled the death as suicide.

In that moment, her first thought, her first word, had been 'impossible'. Her view hadn't changed in the weeks since. Evidence of gunshot residue on his hand, his fingerprints on the bullets and gun, and an unpleasant news article on his desk about the upcoming legislative session hadn't fooled her. Contrary to how the police interpreted the scene, she knew there was a more sinister explanation. There had to be. Unfortunately no one agreed with her.

Had everyone forgotten that Senator Jefferson Daniel Clayton had never taken the coward's way out of any crisis? He'd never backed down from a fight. And even if she was wrong about those two points, she knew beyond all doubt her father would never have disgraced the family home or tainted her childhood memories by killing himself in his study. While she couldn't deny he'd been troubled recently by things he didn't discuss with her, that didn't mean he'd somehow snapped or given in to an undisclosed depression diagnosis as the media and their unnamed sources claimed.

Jana had a copy of her father's letter, urging her discretion and she kept it with her at all times. For her, it was confirmation he'd been killed by someone smart enough and hateful enough to pin the blame on him. While she'd spent too many hours since that first terrible phone call outlining a theory the police would take seriously, she'd made little progress. In fact, the tone of her father's letter and her subsequent research had her paranoid that she was being followed.

She scalded the tip of her tongue on the first sip of her pumpkin spice latte, keeping an eye on the door. Taking a deep breath, she willed herself to remain calm. Any second now, the cavalry would arrive in the form of someone she'd hired to listen to her murder theory and to help her find her father's killer.

Would it be the man in a polo shirt and khakis with the leather portfolio in hand and blue tooth device at his ear? Maybe a woman, she thought as a brunette in a sharp, black pantsuit walked in. Right behind that woman, a man in a wheelchair approached the coffee shop, thanking a lanky cowboy with a wide, friendly smile for an assist with the door.

She didn't know who to expect. Dylan Parker, the name of the contact provided by the Guardian Agency hadn't been gender specific. She'd been informed someone would show up to discuss her concerns and to protect her while ferreting out the truth. One minute she thought the protection wasn't necessary and the next—when she felt like the man in the sport coat across the street was watching her—she latched onto the idea with more enthusiasm.

Deliberately distracting herself, Jana shrugged out of her coat and reached into her purse to silence her phone for the meeting. Seeing a missed call alert from Gregory Atkins, the man who had wanted to marry her, she cleared the history without listening to the message. Though he had been, and still was, more than willing to hear her say "I do," Gregory refused to listen to her murder theory. She could never be with a man who wouldn't at least hear her out on important issues.

Blinking away tears over the sting of that betrayal, she pulled on the frayed edges of her composure. Not even a hired investigator would listen if she blubbered incoherently through her story.

"Ms. Clayton?"

She looked up, mustering a smile for the lanky cowboy who'd walked into the shop a few minutes ago. "Yes?"

"Don't mean to interrupt." With his free hand, he leaned on the chair opposite her. "I'm sorry about your dad."

"Thank you." In addition to that stunning smile, the man had gorgeous, kind eyes. What was she thinking? "I appreciate your condolences. If you'll pardon me, I'm expecting someone any moment now."

"Glad to hear it." He set his coffee cup on the table and removed his hat. "That'd be me. Dylan Parker, at your service."

He extended his hand and, going solely on years of manners and breeding, she responded in kind. Could this man really be the investigator she was waiting for? She'd been sure the unconventional help she'd requested would arrive in more professional attire, like a dark suit or a nondescript trench coat. Those images were spy novel cliché, of course, but she hadn't expected such a casual presentation.

Her promised contact had arrived wearing a faded field jacket over a blue plaid shirt, with dark blue jeans and scuffed cowboy boots. She counted the freshly cut blond hair as a positive. The arresting blue eyes... well, the intensity there proved more convincing than his use of the name that had been messaged to her earlier today along with the time and place of their meeting.

"*You're* Mr. Dylan Parker?"

"Dylan's fine," he said, sitting down in the chair opposite her.

Wait, this wasn't right somehow. This investigation was immensely important and he simply wasn't what she'd had in mind. "I think there's been a mistake." It was a rude assessment, but despite the matching name she couldn't see how this laid-back cowboy would be of any help.

"I get it. I'm not what you expected?" He leaned forward, lowering his voice. "Happens to me all the time. Usually, it works to the client's benefit. Why don't you fill me in on what's going on?"

Here it was, the point of no return. As ready, as eager as she'd been, she hesitated now. What if this was the wrong move? She'd run across the Guardian Agency during a search for a private investigator that would come to Austin and listen with an objective ear. She needed someone who could help her bring a killer to justice.

"I need help, but everyone in town is too connected," she began, and then paused to take a deep breath.

"No one is impartial, everyone in town has an agenda—political or otherwise," he finished for her. "The transcript from your contact email is part of your file."

That he knew what she'd put in her email did little to settle her nerves. Suddenly, her carefully planned recitation of events since her father's death flew out of her head, replaced by a jumble of thoughts rooted in paranoia. She glanced out the window, noticing the man in the sport coat had moved down the block, but not out of sight. Was she being an idiot? Could she afford *not* to talk to this man?

He raised his coffee cup, his eyes serious as he gazed at her over the rim. "You're having second thoughts." He took a long sip, then returned the cup to the table. "If you've changed your mind about the agency or my services I can recommend—"

"No." She thought of the letter and the latest media rumors. She had to do this for the sake of her father's reputation and for her peace of mind. "If you have the transcript of my email you know my prevailing theory."

"I'd like to hear it in your own words."

What were all the questions about? A test to see if her story changed? She supposed even high-end agencies were likely approached with absurd requests from time to time. Reminding herself that the authorities had quickly dismissed her murder theory, she poured out the whole story, keeping her voice low enough to avoid being overheard.

When she finished, Mr. Parker considered her for a long moment. She resisted the urge to squirm under the scrutiny of his penetrating gaze.

"Let me get this straight." His blue eyes collided with hers, as tangible as a touch. "You think someone shot your dad in his study at home and staged the suicide."

"Yes." No matter that his voice was hardly more than a whisper, Jana surveyed the crowded coffee shop. "This isn't the place to discuss these details," she murmured. Ready to bolt, she gripped the strap of her purse. This whole situation was a bad idea.

"In my experience," he said, drawing her attention back to him, "new clients prefer to meet in a public place."

She wouldn't argue, he would know. Still, meeting here felt wrong. "Let's go for a walk." She stood, gathered her coat and purse, and sent a farewell wave to the staff behind the counter.

"Works for me." He pushed back his chair and settled his hat on his head.

At the door, he held it open for her much as he had for the man in the wheelchair. "Who do you suspect?" he asked once they were outside.

Out of habit, she turned toward the state house. Her heart clutched, but she refused to retreat. She had to look at the building without an emotional breakdown or she'd never survive the necessary return to her dad's offices. Grateful for the bright sunshine, she used her sunglasses to shield her grief. Her career—present and future—was tied to that building.

"That's the problem. No one with access to his study had any reason to want him dead."

"That you've found," Mr. Parker countered. "You're a smart lady, Ms. Clayton. You didn't take this step just to have coffee with me this afternoon. Give me whatever you're holding back."

"I don't know what you mean," she evaded. With his good looks and brash approach he'd be a more authentic lobbyist than a private investigator. "You said you read the transcript."

"I did. Which is why I believe you're holding back. Your story is compelling, but what detail in particular *made* you call the agency?"

Well, he was observant, she'd give him that. "I mentioned my concerns to my stepmother." Even now, her stepmother's reaction stung. "I recognize she's over-wrought. I really do. I just can't comprehend how she seems to find the explanation of suicide preferable to murder."

"Takes all kinds of people in this world," he said. "Her reaction probably didn't make you happy, but I doubt it made you decide your dad had been murdered."

Jana hadn't expected sympathy or coddling, but she hadn't expected to feel so... challenged. If she had any substantial leads, she wouldn't need his help. As soon as she got back to her car, she intended to send an email that terminated what had clearly been a foolish idea.

DYLAN HAD MADE up his mind. He'd been down this road before. This was a simple case of wishful thinking. Jana Clayton was a devastated daughter unable to let go of her sparkling image of a perfect daddy. She didn't want to believe the man had killed himself, didn't want to accept the hard reality that people from all walks of life kept sharp, unpleasant secrets hidden beneath the surface.

He had reviewed everything in the file, which included all articles the media had printed since Senator Clayton's body had been found. A single gunshot to the head wasn't the prettiest way to go, but it was effective. And it was, more often than not, exactly what it appeared: suicide.

In the café he'd seen the fresh grief shadowing her moss-green eyes. Despite the expert touch with cosmetics, the puffy, dark circles and skin sallow from lack of sleep were impossible to miss. In another situation, Dylan thought she'd be quite a looker—if she let down the hair she had yanked back into that tight bun. Well, he actually knew she was damned gorgeous under different circumstances since the background file included her history of winning almost as many beauty pageants as academic accolades in her college days.

On top of that, she was distracted, more concerned with the people walking by than giving him the straight story. She was all torn up and not thinking straight. He'd braced to some degree for her emotional state, since her father's life, death, and memorial had all been a public affair. Hell, the senator had only been buried two days ago. The whole scene made Dylan's skin itch as if he'd rolled around in poison ivy. He wanted to snap his fingers, get right in her face, and just blurt out the hard truth. People did dumb, inexplicable things every day of the week. They performed thoughtless, unforgivable acts with no regard for the fallout. Her father had killed himself and made life a misery for those he'd left behind.

Sad but true. The only way to go on was to just go on. He'd learned it firsthand, hadn't he? In a perfect world, he'd still be upholding the law in Montana instead of rattling around the Texas-Louisiana region taking on unique private security assignments like Jana Clayton.

Bottom line, whatever her daddy had done, however emotional and unfocused she was, Jana was smart, too. Before he called it a day and saved her from throwing away her money, he wanted to hear the thing she was holding back. He had an idea what it was.

"He left a letter, didn't he?" Dylan suggested as they walked aimlessly up the block. "Some personal kind of note or message that worries you?"

She glanced at him, but looked away just as quickly. The file and photo had come through yesterday with the standing order to protect her. He could do that and count it easy money. After all, he was overdue for a low-key assignment. Austin was a fun town and Jana was easy on the eyes. But first, she had to tell him *everything*. Holding back would only create trouble for both of them.

When her silence went on, he stopped at the next corner, letting other people pass by. "You asked for help, remember?" He didn't know how she'd found the Guardian Agency, but it only worked one way. Potential clients reached out to them. There were no ads in phone books or on billboards, no business cards passed out at networking meetings.

"I did." She gave a tiny nod as she reached into that deep well of a purse. "I made a copy of the letter." She produced a folded sheet of paper.

He raised his eyebrows. "Why make a copy?"

Her shoulders hitched and she turned her head toward the opposite side of the street. "I want to keep the original... safe."

He unfolded the single page and read the hand-written letter.

Sweetheart,

I've loved you from the moment you took your first breath, before that, though I was too young to realize it was possible at the time. Your miraculous arrival only solidified my commitment to be an honorable man, to provide your every need, and more importantly, to be a father worthy of your love and devotion. The day you joined my staff was one of the proudest of my life. Your insight, intelligence, and perseverance will see you through and propel your career in whichever direction you choose.

You have your mother's eyes along with her conviction and dedication to a worthy purpose. As you're well aware, she was - and remains - my inspiration, the solid foundation of my personal and political decisions. If a decision would make her shake her head at me, I re-think it and find another way.

You're also well aware that politics can get ugly, even for your dad. In the coming weeks, a little mud might fly my way. You can't believe it. In fact, you must not believe it. Whatever happens, whatever wild claims are launched, however the public reacts, I want you to hold your head high, to know that I remain steadfast, worthy of your faith and admiration as both my daughter and as a valued part of my political team.

If you find cause to doubt me, don't doubt your mother's ever-present and ongoing influence over me. I know I've been preoccupied and aloof in recent months, but that was to protect you from a flood of trouble I may not be able to stop. However this letter finds you, I beg you to keep it to yourself. You mustn't trust anyone else, only yourself and your flawless intuition. Be safe, be smart, and above all continue to be the amazing woman I admire.

Love you like crazy,

Daddy

Dylan read through the letter a second time, folded it, and tucked it into his back pocket for further evaluation. "You're sure he wrote this?"

"Yes."

She had clearly read the letter from a differing perspective. For Dylan, the words painted a clear picture—her father was seriously worried about something or someone. But that didn't mean he hadn't opted to make an untimely exit. "He didn't want you trusting anyone. How will you trust me?" Before she could answer, he added, "If you still want my help, trust will be an important part of our relationship, Ms. Clayton."

Her full lips thinned to a flat line. Frustration? Second thoughts? Dylan couldn't wait to hear her response.

"When I received the letter, I knew I'd been right in my conclusion about his death. That said, it seemed prudent to find an objective third party to confirm or disprove my theory. I'm trusting your integrity as well as that of your agency, Mr. Parker."

Fancy way to say she was scared and not sure what the hell she should feel or do. "Do you ever relax, Ms. Clayton?"

"I beg your pardon?"

"You should. Relax I mean," he clarified, shifting closer as they started walking again. "You're wound tight. It's understandable in these circumstances, but if you took a step back, stop operating on emotion, you might see—"

"That's enough." She pushed her sunglasses to the top of her head. "My personal life isn't up for evaluation or debate."

Whoa. He'd hit a hot button there. "No, it isn't." He liked the way her soft green eyes turned sharp with temper. It showed him some conviction under all that sorrow. "I'd apologize for being out of line, but it goes with the job. You said you wanted help getting to the truth about your dad. Could it be you're ignoring the obvious answer?"

She stopped between two storefronts, and planted her hands on her hips. "That is *not* a suicide letter. It's a warning, not a farewell. If my dad had ever considered taking his own life, it would've been years ago when we lost my mother." She paused, gulping air.

Her mother's death over fifteen years ago had been in her file, along with other notable details and public records for the Clayton family. As an outsider looking in, it would be easy to agree with her assessment. Senator Clayton had been in politics long enough to sink hip-deep in scandal, but somehow he'd stayed above the worst of the muck and mud-slinging. Other than her mother's death, the family had all the earmarks of the perfect life: power, money, and, more importantly, respect—at least until now.

"Yes, I'm grieving," she continued, "but I haven't lost touch with reality. No one knew my father better than I did. The evidence points to suicide because someone wanted it to."

"You've got the clout to push the police to look at the situation more closely."

"I need an objective assessment before I start pushing anyone." She stepped back, scowling at him before she hid her eyes with the sunglasses again.

"Just in case you're wrong," he tossed back at her.

Her posture stiffened. "I am *not* wrong. I need an objective assessment for my stepmother... for the police. And... I think someone might be following me."

His instincts sharpened. "You didn't feel it was important to mention that detail until now?"

"I... I can't be sure. Admittedly, I'm overtired. It might just be a reporter looking for dirt, a fresh angle, or an inside story."

Scanning the crowd and the street, he made up his mind then and there. Whether her father killed himself or not, there was something off here and he intended to learn what that something was. "Whatever else you believe, I'm here to protect you, Ms. Clayton, until you fire me or I'm ordered otherwise."

"A bodyguard isn't what I requested. I need an investigator."

He gave her a smile, hoping to ease the tension. The lady looked ready to snap. "Two in one deal, that's how we do it."

She folded her arms. "Can you be of any help in an investigative capacity?"

He nodded, not taking her question as a personal affront. "I expect my resume would surprise you."

"Everything else has," she muttered. "So, how will this work?"

He swallowed his amusement, adjusting his hat against the glint of the sun. "You have a choice," he began. "I can act more like a protective detail—"

"The bodyguard I don't need?"

"That's right. Or we can come up with a better reason why I'm suddenly with you twenty-four-seven."

"A bodyguard raises questions I don't want to answer."

"Worried it makes you look paranoid, like suicide is contagious?"

"That isn't what I meant and it's rude."

"It is," he agreed. "You've spent enough time in the spotlight to know how harsh the media can be. We have to see this the way they do."

"Are you this insensitive with all of your clients?"

"I'm not your best friend or your therapist. I protect and investigate," he replied, pleased to have heard more curiosity than irritation in her voice. He'd take both over the other fluttery, runaway emotions she'd displayed so far. "I do what needs to be done, Ms. Clayton."

"Jana," she corrected firmly. "If we're to make it believable, how about this? It's been a long time since our college days, but I'm glad you're here to lend me a shoulder to cry on, Dylan. Thank you."

He tried not to wince at her choice of cover stories. These days his shoulders were only for him and physical contact happened on his terms or not at all. He didn't encourage friendly displays of affection until he was sure the woman wouldn't sprout prickly expectations. While he never allowed things to get personal with a client, he knew there was a time and place to play a role. For her sake and for the people who seemed to track her every move, he had to give her points for creativity.

"Anything you need," he replied. *On a professional level*, he amended silently. Protecting her didn't mean he had to listen to tear-soaked trips down memory lane. "Where to first?"

"Let's start with Dad's office at the state house." Her hand disappeared into her purse and she pulled out a car key fob as they started walking again. "There had to be something he was working on that set this nightmare in motion. I need to find it."

"Where did you park?" Dylan asked, knowing the answer. He'd been watching the coffee shop for her arrival and getting a feel for the area.

"Over on Sixth."

He caught the little hitch in her breath as they

turned away from the view of the capitol building. He marveled at his bad luck, getting stuck with this case. Jana Clayton seemed nice enough, but dealing with raw emotions weren't part of his skill set. He'd turned those off after his ex-wife stuck half a dozen daggers in his back. Some men used alcohol to drown their heartache. Others used their damaged feelings as a reason to be jerks. Dylan decided it was just easier to stop feeling at all. Made life a lot simpler.

The deep, throaty roar of an engine caught his attention. Instinctively, he stepped in front of Jana as a dark blur of a motorcycle rushed around the corner. Sunlight bounced off black helmets with dark visors and the riders wore black down to their boots. The driver leaned forward as the passenger raised an automatic pistol. Dylan pushed Jana to the ground, sheltering her body with his, while he watched the inevitable unfold.

Bright muzzle flashes and the gleam of chrome accents on the bike broke up the black mass attacking them. Screams of panicked civilians echoed around them, punctuating the sounds of the engine, gunfire, and breaking glass. The motorcycle weaved in and out of traffic and then disappeared down North Congress, gone long before the first emergency call could be made.

Dylan helped Jana to her feet. "Are you okay?"

"I'm fine." She dusted off her palms and hefted her purse back to her shoulder. "What about you?"

"I'm good." He looked her over again before urging her away from the scene. The only damage appeared to be her broken sunglasses and dirt from the sidewalk on her knees and palms. "We should get to your car."

"We need to help the others," Jana argued. "The police will need our statements."

He shook his head, catching her arm. "It's not safe."

She stopped short and stared him down. "People may be hurt."

"It's your life I'm here to protect."

"I'm not leaving. We stay and help where we can."

Dylan bit back an oath. He should be grateful she wasn't in shock or crying. "What about getting to your dad's office?"

"That can wait." She was already moving down the street, wading into the chaos.

His only choice was to follow her. *This time.* Staying as close as her shadow, he watched, reluctantly impressed as she checked on one person after another, soothing those with minor injuries.

As hard as it was to believe, no one had been seriously injured. By the time the authorities and emergency medical teams arrived, Dylan had studied the path of the bullets. The main cluster seemed to be right where he and Jana had been standing.

This case had just gone from a daughter's denial to a potential murder investigation. Jana had been right to believe someone was watching her. He took a few pictures of the chewed up wall with his cell and sent them to his tech and research assistant Claudia. His experience in law enforcement had him itching to pick up a shell casing, but that would take him too far from his client. It was possible the goal hadn't been to kill her, but to create a serious diversion and to possibly kidnap her. Snapping pictures of people milling around, he stood with Jana as they gave their statements to the police. The moment they were cleared to go, he guided her toward their cars.

"The police aren't going to find anything," he said, waiting for her to fish out her car key again.

"How can you be so sure?"

"That was a professional hit."

Her eyes went wide then she shook her head. "That's ridiculous. It had to be a random crime. Austin is for the most part a wonderful city, but we have the typical urban issues with drugs and gangs."

He shrugged off her doubt. She didn't know any better, that's why he was here. "We need to get off the street." His instincts were humming, urging him to take her somewhere less exposed.

She fisted her hand over her car key, but not before he saw the way it shook. "I'll meet you at the state house parking garage."

Not what he had in mind. In his professional opinion, she needed some privacy and a little time to regroup before they discussed what the hell just happened. "I should take you home."

"Absolutely not." She glowered at him. "I refuse to let a random act of violence dictate my schedule. My father wouldn't…" Her renewed fury died as swiftly as it had appeared.

He took her car key. "We'll talk about going to the office after I take you home."

CHAPTER 2

JANA COULDN'T QUITE BELIEVE she'd relinquished so much control to Mr. Parker. He'd nudged her into the passenger seat of her own car and then, rather than take her to the capitol building as she'd requested, he'd driven to her house and urged her to take a minute and clean up. When she'd caught her reflection in the hall mirror, she could only be grateful for his discretion.

Miraculously no one had been critically injured, but the drive-by shooting left her more than a little rattled. Her face smudged with dirt, her hair falling in wisps and chunks from the chignon at her nape, pants torn and palms scraped, she looked a mess. Showing up to Senator Clayton's office like this would give the media gossips fodder for months, shattering the polished image she'd worked long and hard to culti-vate. Though she wasn't quite thirty, she was old enough to serve out her father's senate term, and while doing so would accelerate her plans for a political career, she wouldn't turn down the appointment. Her father would want her to finish all he'd started. The only way to ensure that happened was to step up to the plate.

Had Mr. Parker recognized that showing up in disarray would give her future opponents ammunition and a visible example of bad judgment? She should've thought of that, and would have if she wasn't so confused and overwhelmed. The images on the news of her at the scene would have the reporters nipping even more closely at her heels. The images playing through her mind had far worse implications.

She hadn't seen much beyond Mr. Parker's shirt as he'd stepped between her and the gunfire and the police likely couldn't do much with her statement, but she'd had to try. Now, relaxing in her favorite yoga pants and an oversized t-shirt, she sipped the cup of tea Mr. Parker had encouraged—ordered, actually—her to make. The concept that the shooting had been a professional hit kept creeping into her other whirling thoughts. Surely he'd been wrong. Why would anyone want to kill her?

Maybe the same person who murdered her father…

"How're you feeling?" he asked, settling into the chair across from her. He looked distinctly out of place in her front room surrounded by the subtle feminine décor.

"Fine," she lied. If she let go of the cup, her hands would start trembling again. "Thank you, Mr. Parker."

"Dylan," he reminded her. "We need to start acting like we're old friends."

He was right. "Okay." With his good looks and

tendency to speak candidly, she would've enjoyed a friend like him at any point in her past.

Sitting here thinking of the answers she'd have to provide for the inevitable questions about the shooting left her exhausted. Her colleagues as well as the media would need answers. Maybe she wasn't as strong as she wanted to believe. Her father had been so robust, so vital and steady through every crisis and she... she clearly wasn't. Her heart still raced. Sitting here with Dylan watching her so intently wasn't helping.

"If you have other things to do," she suggested, "I'll be fine now. I can meet you at my father's offices in an hour."

"I need to pick up my truck, but I'm not about to leave you here alone."

That was ridiculous. "It's a gated community and I have a security system." She stared at his serious face as he did something with his phone. The shooting couldn't have been about her. "I'm sure we were just in the wrong place at the wrong time," she added, more to herself than to him.

"You hired an expert." He tapped his chest. "Trust the expert." Crossing the room, he sat beside her on the couch. "Here are the pictures I took right after the drive-by. Scroll through and take your time." He held out his phone. "Let me know if anyone looks familiar."

She set aside her mug of tea and fisted her hands, reluctant to allow them to quake like those of a frightened child in front of 'the expert'. Taking his phone, she studied each picture, hearing the gunfire and noise all over again as she saw the shock and fear stamped on every face caught in each frame. The man she'd thought had been following her wasn't in any of the pictures. She couldn't recall seeing him after her meeting with Dylan started.

"I don't recognize anyone."

"You said you thought someone had been following you."

"Maybe he's a reporter." She shrugged. "Either way, he's not in the pictures." The idea sounded paranoid even to her.

Dylan set the phone on the coffee table. "Were you and your dad working on something in particular that you believe prompted hard feelings toward him or you?"

The question shouldn't have startled her. Her father was dead and she was convinced he was murdered. Yet, somehow it did. "This time of year it's mostly committee work, charity events, and a bit of maneuvering in anticipation of the next session."

"It's not my world," he admitted. "Let's try another avenue. With your father dead, who might want you out of the way?"

She shook her head. The idea was ridiculous. "I don't have enemies like that. My father was the one with the power. I have people with differing opinions on issues, but no actual enemies." Had her father really had enemies willing to stoop to murder to get what they wanted?

Make up your mind, Jana. He was either murdered or…

"Staging a suicide in a man's own home is personal and risky," Dylan pointed out. "If your father was murdered, there must be one hell of a motive for the killer to take a risk like that."

Her stomach pitched. Hiring an investigator was supposed to make this easier, instead she found herself tumbling deeper into confusion and uncertainty. If her dad committed suicide, then she'd failed him by ignoring a cry for help. If he was murdered, it was by someone close enough to get into the study. Which made her naïve and gullible for trusting anyone.

But did any of it make her a potential victim? "I just don't know." She let go a big breath. "I'm sorry. I can't seem to think straight."

"We'll figure it out," he promised. "One step at a time. Right now we need to pick up my truck." He braced his hands on his knees and pushed to his feet. "Let's go."

"I'll be fine here," she protested. Tears were clogging her throat again. "It's perfectly safe here." She stared out the window, praying for nightfall when she could stand outside in the dark and pretend she was anyone but Jana Clayton. As strange as it sounded, since she was a teenager she had found the anonymity of darkness healing somehow.

"You mean, like your father's study? I'm certain he felt completely safe there."

Her lips trembled in spite of her best efforts. The man knew how to draw blood.

"Staying here alone isn't an option," he said. "We're together until this is resolved."

"Mr. Parker," she began, but he cut her off with a

pointed look. "Dylan." She sighed. "What if I call another friend to wait with me?"

He settled his hat into place and ran his hands over the brim. "Would this be an armed friend with experience in personal security?"

She sighed. "No."

He shook his head slowly from side to side. "The sooner we go, the sooner you're home again. I'm not taking any unnecessary chances with your safety. The cab should be here shortly."

She recognized the determination in the hard set of his jaw and the glint in his eyes. Arguing with him was a waste of time. Her home phone rang, interrupting the tense moment. She glanced at the caller ID and groaned. She ignored the call from her father's chief of staff, Samuel Maguire. He must have seen the breaking news report and she wasn't ready to talk about the shooting with anyone else just now. If the call was urgent, he would try her cell. Even as the thought formed, her cell phone rang. She ignored that, too, slipping on tennis shoes for the mandatory field trip to get Mr. Parker's—Dylan's truck.

Her arms and legs ached. How could she be so sore from merely falling to the ground? As she picked up her purse, reaching inside for her house keys, the supple leather shifted revealing a small hole. She stared at it, a new kind of shock settling over her. "I guess they got closer than I realized." Her hands trembling, she showed the hole to Dylan.

"Maybe we caught a break," he said. "Let me have a closer look."

Damn it, she liked this purse. She carefully removed each item inside and placed it on the coffee table. She grimaced at the sight of a bullet burrowed into her grandmother's antique silver compact. "Should we call the police?"

"It's probably useless for prints," Dylan said, "but I'll take care of it. Do you have a plastic baggie?"

"Sure." She went to the kitchen and brought one back. He took a picture of the offensive slug with his phone, then used the baggie to seal away both her compact and the bullet.

For long minutes she just stared, letting the reality sink in. Someone had nearly shot her today. She had wanted to believe it was random, but what if Dylan hadn't been there?

"Cab's here," he said gently as if he realized where her thoughts had gone.

She grabbed her phone and left the rest of the mess on the coffee table for later. They didn't speak in the cab and she was more than a little grateful that he chose the radio over conversation in the truck on the drive back to her house. Her head was spinning. She had been certain her father would never commit suicide. But now she had evidence... sort of. She should be thankful, but mostly she felt unsteady.

When they arrived back at her home, he walked her inside and ordered her to wait in the foyer while he searched the house. She'd activated the security system. He'd watched her disarm it when they came inside. Impatience nipped at her, but she was too drained to argue.

"You'll be okay tonight?" he asked reaching past her to the front door.

She nodded when what she really wanted to do was shake her head. She wasn't so sure she would ever be okay again. "Where are you staying?" The question couldn't have sounded any more needy.

His lips twitched at one corner as if he could see straight into her worry-filled soul. "I'll be on duty outside. You have my number if there's trouble. I entered it into your cell. What time do you want to get started in the morning? I'll be doing the driving."

Outside? This felt ridiculous. She could just imagine the complaints from her neighbors if they noticed a stranger loitering about. Worse, her hope for a few minutes of unobserved peace in the darkness evaporated. "I can drive myself to the office," she said. She'd been doing so for years. "Don't you have a hotel?"

"Stand down, Jana, and let me do my job."

She didn't like the way he kept her off balance, unyielding one minute, and marginally considerate the next, and then totally obstinate again. "I like my alone time." Her private time was scarce. She didn't like giving up what little she managed to carve out.

"Do you have everything you need for tonight?" he asked, ignoring her frustration.

Not only had he ignored her protests, he hadn't answered her question about where he would be. "Yes. Yes, I have everything I need."

"All right. We'll start fresh in the morning."

He made it sound so reasonable, but she suddenly didn't know what to do with the rest of the night. No, that wasn't true. She abruptly felt alone... and afraid. "Where will you be?"

"Right outside," he assured her. "Now, pull the curtains and put in a movie. You need a good night's rest."

He was out the door before she could come up with an intelligent reply. She locked the door behind him and leaned against it for a moment. On a normal evening there would be briefs to read, news reports to review, possibly dinner or drinks with colleagues or friends. The thought of tackling just one of those items brought her to the brink of tears. Work had never made her weepy.

Reluctantly admitting Dylan might have a point, she turned off her cell phone and headed to her bedroom. She played back those brief seconds on the sidewalk again and again. He'd reacted, pushing her down before the first bullets had ripped through the air. Was he that good or was it possible he'd set up the stunt to scare her into relying on him?

That possibility felt all wrong, but what did she know about any of it? She dropped her head into her hands, fingertips digging into her scalp. She thought of her father's letter and the line about trusting her intuition. As foolhardy as it might be, she sensed that Dylan Parker was exactly who and what he said he was. At the moment, there was no one else she could turn to.

After she'd washed her face and brushed her teeth, she added an extra layer of cream under her eyes. Feeling chilled from head to toe, she pulled on some thick socks and slipped under the covers, not bothering to change out of her clothes.

Closing her eyes, she willed herself to stay calm and to stay put until morning.

The cavalry was here... even if Dylan Parker wasn't at all what she'd expected.

GRATEFUL FOR THE DARKNESS, Dylan climbed into his truck and closed the door. It was early, barely eight-thirty. He hoped Jana would get some rest. She was little use to the investigation if she couldn't think straight or keep her emotions in check. Although he hadn't gone through the loss of a parent and didn't want to belittle her grief, he needed her focused. Keeping her that way was going to be a challenge.

He dragged his cell phone from his pocket and sent an update to Claudia. Claudia was his only connection to the Guardian Agency. Whatever he needed, Claudia made it happen. He wondered what she would say if he told her he needed out of this assignment. Hell, he wasn't a quitter, but Jana Clayton needed more of the things he couldn't give her—like a shoulder to cry on and someone to hold her close. He'd barely resisted taking her into his arms after the drive-by. He never did that! Never let a female client—a woman period—make him feel the need to hold and soothe and comfort. The only time he touched a client was to protect that person from danger.

What was it about this woman that made him want

to reach out and draw her in? She was a couple of years younger than him, his sister's age. She was strong, like his sister and his mother. Parker women were a strong lot. Maybe that familiarity was the draw. Jana Clayton was strong, sure, and determined. And none of that mattered.

Dylan dropped his cell on the seat and eased into a more comfortable position. Funny thing was he typically preferred a sweet, come-rescue-me type of woman.

"And just look where that got you, Parker."

Relieved from duty. Arrested. And an empty bank account. He'd lost everything because he'd played hero and rescued the wrong woman. He'd been so damned sure he was in love. Lust had been more like it. Along with that rescue-me attitude, his ex had been gorgeous. Maybe he'd held that against Jana from the moment he read her file. After all, she had won a damned bunch of those beauty pageants just like his ex. Truth was, Jana kept surprising him.

She was classy and smart... and beautiful. And he was *not* interested in her as a person.

He was here for the job. To protect her. To determine *if* her father was murdered.

He thought of his sister and his mother, two women he loved and respected. If either of them needed help that he for some reason couldn't provide, he would want the person who came to their rescue to do the job right.

Whether her father had committed suicide or had been murdered... whether the drive-by was just someone trying to scare her away from that scenario, Jana Clayton deserved for his best effort here.

Forcing his mind to the case file rather than the subject under his protection, he wondered if maybe he shouldn't do a little extra leg work. Claudia was a miracle worker, no doubt, but personal connections were also essential.

He picked up his phone and looked up the number for Hank Patterson, former SEAL and founder of the Brotherhood Protectors. Dylan had learned about Patterson and the new team he was assembling back when he'd worked in Montana. Before his life had fallen apart.

He ignored the sting of old memories and hit the icon to make the call.

"Patterson."

Dylan sat up straight, startled to get the man himself rather than a receptionist or assistant. He quickly introduced himself as a bodyguard. "I'm here in Texas getting rolling on a protection case for the daughter of a state senator."

"Clayton?" Patterson asked.

"You knew him?"

"Saw it on the news," Hank said. "Austin is a bit outside of my usual neighborhood."

"Yeah, but your reputation precedes you. Do you have anyone in this area I might call on in case I need a trustworthy backup?"

Hank might have laughed. Or snorted. "Thought Guardian worked you guys as a solo act."

"Autonomous," Dylan said with a smile. With Hank's

connections and clientele, he shouldn't be surprised that Patterson knew of the agency. "I've got all the background and research help I need. Normally it wouldn't cross my mind to ask for another pair of boots on the ground, but something here isn't right and the woman is a public figure."

"That she is." Dylan figured Hank was searching the web for Jana and the latest details on the situation. "You dodged a drive-by already?"

"Assuming it's related," Dylan replied.

Hank murmured something Dylan couldn't quite make out. "I've got a man who can get down there and keep an eye on your six. Goes by Swede. I'll text you his number."

"Thanks, man. I'll send you the address for the bill."

With Hank's low laughter in his ear, he ended the call and sank deeper into his seat. Though he still couldn't identify a specific threat, he felt better already.

THURSDAY, *November 15*

"Jana?"

The deep, gentle voice woke her with a start. "Dylan!" She sat up and looked from the man in her bedroom doorway to the clock. Seeing how late she'd overslept, she hopped out of bed. "What are you doing in my house?"

"You didn't answer your phone."

"I turned it off to get some rest." Her heart hammered against her ribs. She needed to get her bearings. "How did you get in here?" She should've heard something. She pushed at her hair, glancing at the security system panel by her bedroom door. It was oddly silent.

"Through the garage. You didn't set your alarm."

She always set her security alarm. Searching her memory of last night, she straightened her twisted clothing. So maybe she did forget. She cleared her throat, uncertain of the protocol for this situation. Were all bodyguards this bold? He was in her bedroom, looking ready to tackle the day in a crisp oxford shirt and jeans.

"You can't be in here."

"I needed to confirm you weren't injured," he said, a hot lick of impatience in his voice.

Nothing injured but her pride. "You can wait in the kitchen while I dress."

"Do you want me to start breakfast?"

Was he serious? "No! I mean, that's not necessary," she added with more control. She couldn't eat now if she wanted to. Embarrassment was giving way to irritation over what felt like his increasing violations of her privacy. She didn't like this. "Give me fifteen minutes."

"Take all the time you need." He stepped back from her bedroom doorway. "I'll brew coffee."

Tempting as that sounded, she wouldn't give him a moment longer than necessary to poke around her house. She assumed investigators were prone to snooping and while she didn't have any secrets, that didn't mean she wanted him digging through her life. She rushed through her morning routine in record time and hurried to the kitchen to find him leaning against her counter, legs crossed at the ankle.

He raised his mug of coffee. "Good morning, sunshine."

"Don't say things like that." They barely knew each other. He was far too forward.

"Why not? It's a habit I picked up from my mom."

"No offense to your mom." Jana had no idea what to do with remarks like that, delivered with such casual confidence. "Endearments like that are too familiar."

"Even for old college friends?"

What had seemed like a good idea yesterday didn't feel so much like one today. "Coffee." It was the only safe response. Caffeine would get her brain firing on all cylinders. She headed for the cabinet where she stored travel mugs and filled one, leaving space for sugar and a splash of cream. "I really don't appreciate you coming into my house unannounced."

His gaze locked with hers. "I called. You didn't answer. I knocked and rang the bell. You didn't answer. I let myself in to check on you, per the job you hired me for. That's all." He tipped his head toward the coffee pot. "Except for that."

Okay, so she couldn't take exception with him doing his job. She took a long swallow of her coffee. He stared at her, those intense eyes analyzing, though his lips quirked as if he was holding back a smile.

"Why are you looking at me that way?"

"What way?" He sipped his coffee, clearly amused.

"As if you're enjoying a joke at my expense." She did not like this feeling. She did not like him catching her in bed. Whatever truce they had reached last night, she suddenly felt back at square one.

"I'm just thinking, you don't seem the type to oversleep."

She reminded herself that excellent observation skills were an asset in his line of work. "You'd be right about that." It surprised her to realize that despite the abrupt and inappropriate wake up call, she'd slept well enough to feel refreshed. "At any rate, can we go?"

"Don't you want something to eat first?"

"No." She pressed a hand to her stomach. Sleep was a good start, but her appetite had yet to make a comeback. "I just want to get this over with."

Going through her father's office was going to be damned tough. She'd tried to do this three other times in the past two weeks. First, she simply couldn't. The second time, meetings had gotten in the way. The day before yesterday, Camille had needed her. Nothing and no one was getting in the way this time. Not even herself.

To her surprise, Dylan rinsed out his coffee mug, placed it in the dishwasher, and then shut off the coffeemaker. He snagged her car key from her hand, his fingers brushing hers. "Let's roll."

The tingle that zinged up her arm made her frown. "That's annoying." She was not happy with his insistence on taking control of everything… including her.

"What?" he asked, opening the door to the garage and waiting for her to go ahead of him.

"The way you take charge as if I'm too helpless to do anything for myself."

"I thought opening doors was still the way things were done down here."

She inhaled a deep breath, reached for patience. "Not that. You're far too comfortable with my things. With me," she blurted, unable to contain her frustration. He'd been in her house. He'd caught her sleeping. Making coffee and opening doors wouldn't make up for that kind of familiarity. She didn't like his… presumptuousness.

So why was there a small part of her simply reveling in his every gesture and expression? He'd cleaned up somewhere. The woodsy scent of his body wash teased her nose.

"Goes with the job," he said while he armed the security system. "I make it my business to know everything about my assignment and how best to keep a client safe."

Rather than debate his attitude further and waste even more time, she settled into the passenger seat of her car and kept her annoyance to herself as he backed out of the garage and guided the car onto the street. If— big if—she really had been the target of that shooting, she needed him.

To find her father's killer she needed him.

She had wanted help and he was here. It was time to focus on what she'd hired his agency to do. "When we get to the state house, I'll sign you in as a guest. Anyone who asks will hear the old college friend line."

"Do you work with anyone who knew you in college?"

"Not directly."

He kept his eyes on the traffic.

"You already knew that." Why had he asked if he knew the answer?

"I suspected as much, just confirming."

"How?" She refused to volunteer more information until she had better answers. Her whole life was under public scrutiny day in and day out. Having this man digging into her personal life shouldn't faze her and yet it did. "My social life has nothing to do with my father's murder."

"It could. The Claytons are the equivalent of local celebrities. Like the Kennedys of Austin."

She scoffed at that, directing him into her assigned parking space.

He cut the engine and turned to face her. "It's true. When I'm assigned to a case, I get a photo and a case file. For you, I'm glad it's electronic. Your connections and history, along with your dad's, could fill a library."

"I see." She unbuckled her seat belt. "And did any of that information lead you toward someone who might have motive to murder my father?"

His vivid blue eyes kept her glued to her seat. "I've just started looking. Before that drive-by, I was pretty much convinced your theory was wrong."

Her fingers twitched. She would love nothing more than to slap him. His determination to frustrate her had no bounds. Wasn't there some way for him to hurry up and find her father's killer? Without the truth, she couldn't make the world see her father hadn't let them down. "Let's get this over with, shall we?"

"Hang on." He flipped the key fob into his palm.

"What's our game plan? What exactly are you looking for in the office?"

"I'm not sure," she admitted. "I'm hoping to know it when I see it. There has to be something that will give us a lead. I'm up on every issue he had before him." Unless, as he'd suggested in his letter, he'd kept something hidden from her. On a level too deep to discuss with a stranger, the idea that her father hadn't told her everything hurt more than she could articulate.

"Shouldn't we start with the scene of the crime?"

Jana swallowed back the emotion choking her. Sorrow filled every cell in her body, weighing her down. "I –I'm not sure," she said. Hearing the tears in her voice, seeing his expression turn cool and aloof, she gathered herself. Her personal agony would wait until justice was served. "The police report says no sign of a struggle, no sign of a break in. I think Dad knew his killer, which isn't surprising. After three decades in office, he knew everyone in the state and considered most of them friends. I thought it would be best to start in his office."

The idea that his killer was a close friend was unthinkable. Still, there was no avoiding that possibility. Who else would have gotten close enough to kill him? "He was a good man." She blotted her eyes with a tissue. It hurt to even think of her father in the past tense and as much as she tried to bury her reactions, her emotions floated too close to the surface. "This isn't easy for me. We were very close as a family and closer still after my mother died. I apologize if my grief makes you uncomfortable."

"Don't worry about me," he said with a quick shrug.

She thought of the actions he'd taken in their brief acquaintance, thought of the bullet they'd retrieved from her purse. Despite finding him difficult on a personal level, she needed him. Showing the proper respect to him and gratitude for his assistance was important.

Her father and the honorable legacy he deserved wouldn't tolerate anything less.

She and Dylan were in this together now.

DYLAN WAS miles away from having a lead, but he'd only just started. Whatever there was to find, he would find it. He had to admit that Jana was right about the waterworks making him uncomfortable. Since his ex screwed him over he had zero tolerance for emotional outbursts. Crying didn't get a job done, it only impeded progress.

One way or another he had to get it through his thick skull that Jana wasn't his ex or a potential date, she was his client. She was in a bad place right now and he needed to remember that each time his body longed to comfort her. *Not smart, man.*

He followed her through security, keeping his responses short and friendly as she introduced him to Jerry, the man currently on duty. The woman seemed to know everyone by first name and accepted sympathy and greetings from every person who crossed her path, with the same gracious bravery. Her reactions didn't change, no matter the person's post in the capitol. She'd even asked the janitor about what must have been a traditional Thanksgiving recipe in his family.

Dylan recalculated, changing his opinion of Jana as they made their way up to the senator's office. On paper she was involved with more groups than anyone could be and stay sane. At least from his perspective. Now he realized that long list of interests wasn't merely for show or to give various charities and organizations a political name to drop. Jana Clayton seemed to be the real deal when it came to giving of her time and effort. More surprising, everyone she introduced him to thanked him for coming to lend her support. In his experience, people didn't care that much about anyone unless that care was earned through some investment or personal sacrifice. The file didn't say anything about a significant other or inseparable girlfriend in her life and that struck him as odd. Not that it really mattered. He was only curious about her social life because it might impact his job.

Dangerous territory, Parker.

Her hands trembled as she unlocked the office door, but she squared her shoulders as she walked in. He followed her, locking the door behind them.

"I don't want any surprises," he explained. "This building is busier than I expected this time of year."

"Everyone's preparing for the next legislative session."

He'd never given politics or the legislative process much thought. "I'll start out here, you can go through your dad's things. We're looking for anything that doesn't fit. Is there a particular person or issue that comes to mind?"

Eyes about to spill over again, she shook her head and left the small reception area for her father's office.

Concentrating on the task before him, he surveyed the reception area. The high-end furnishings managed to give off a lived-in feel. There was nothing pretentious about the senator's suite of offices. Dylan turned on the computer at the receptionist's desk, but it was password protected. Taking in the personal pictures scattered about, the military and civilian honors framed on the walls, he thought Senator Clayton had struck a smart balance between bragging rights and credentials that would give visitors confidence.

In the other room, he heard the little hiccups and catches of Jana's sorrow. He took all the time he could with the reception area, but came up empty of anything incriminating or questionable. Damn it. The logical next step was to get in there and help her. In public, he could play the supporting role, but privately, he dreaded it. Too bad. It was time to man up. Gritting his teeth, he trudged in and stopped short.

"Holy hell. What did you do?" She was behind the big executive desk, sitting on the floor under the window, the contents of a large file drawer scattered around her like paper snow drifts.

"The drawer stuck," she said defensively.

The battle had been the quietest fight between a woman and a drawer he'd ever heard. He carefully stepped closer, wary of her since she'd already taken her frustration out on an inanimate object. He dropped to one knee, just out of her reach. "This isn't the best way to conduct a covert search."

"I don't care about covert." Her chin came up, daring him to argue. "I'm looking for the truth."

At this point he hoped to find a stash of whiskey to ease their mutual discomfort. The woman sitting amid the mess on the floor didn't bear any resemblance to a professional going through her father's effects. He picked up the closest file labeled 'personal notes'.

"I've been through that one," she grumbled.

He didn't bother to reply. Quickly, he flipped through handwritten cards and letters from constituents and associates and then returned the file to the desk drawer. After going through a few more he decided either the senator was as respected and beloved as Jana claimed, or the hate mail was filed in another place.

He picked up another file as she finished it, but at her dark look, he simply put it back in the drawer. Choosing to leave her to it, he stood and searched the rest of the office, feeling behind frames and books, under drawers and chairs for anything from a secret catch to a listening device. He checked the air vents as well as anything else that might budge.

The place was clean.

"He wasn't a spy," Jana said when he stood in the middle of the room and gazed up at the light fixture.

Turning, he met her gaze. "Everyone has a skeleton or two in the closet."

"Do tell," she challenged.

He was sorely tempted. If nothing else, his past

might shock her into not being so vulnerable in front of him. "Another time." He considered the thick stack of papers she'd gathered to one side. She'd straightened up the mess quickly. All signs of the earlier paper storm were gone. "Did you find anything helpful?"

She stared forlornly at the stack. "Who knows? Nothing has a red flag with a dire warning or explanation. I'll take a closer look at home."

"Did he ever receive hate mail?" Dylan studied the room again, from the ceiling to the floor. They were missing something.

She nodded. "He and Rose, his receptionist, went through it once a month. It was either trashed or filed."

"Where?" He hadn't seen any kind of file like that in the outer office or in here. "They didn't report it?"

"The few that were filed, he kept in his study. As for reporting any of it, I only remember one time. It was a death threat," Jana said, leading the way back to the reception area. "That was years ago and it turned out to be nothing."

"Tell me again why are you taking all that," he nodded to the pile, "home?"

"Because these are papers he would want me to have. Some are things I need to organize for whoever is appointed to fulfill his term." She sat down at the receptionist's keyboard and entered a password. The desktop monitor lit up with a standard sunset screen saver and one column of file folders marching down the left side.

Dylan leaned over her shoulder as she opened each folder. He had her print out the last few pages of her dad's schedule and tucked the sheets into his back pocket. He was about to ask her to download the contents of another file to his jump drive when a key rattled in the door lock. The noise startled Jana, but he held his position, one hand on the back of her chair as they faced the new arrival.

"Sam!" The name popped out of her a little too brightly. "What are you doing here?"

The older man sent her a strained smile. Dressed casually, he looked like he should be on the golf course rather than in a senator's office.

"Jerry told me you'd come in. With a friend," he added, his dark eyes taking Dylan's measure.

"Sam Maguire, this is a friend of mine from college, Dylan Parker." She turned to Dylan. "Sam is Dad's chief of staff."

"A pleasure," Dylan said, extending a hand. The other man's palm was dry, the grip firm, but his expression and posture didn't come close to friendly.

"Likewise," Sam said. Turning a sympathetic look to Jana, he continued. "You don't have to be in any rush to clean out your dad's office or your own, honey."

She clasped her hands together in her lap and sighed. "I was just trying to wrap up a few loose ends."

"The University of Texas has requested some material," Dylan said, filling the awkward gap. "They're creating a Senator Clayton memorial section in the library."

Sam looked from Dylan to Jana, who nodded quickly. "I see," he said noncommittally.

"Rose kept images of his awards." Jana grabbed the

ball Dylan had lobbed up and ran with it. "I thought that was the most efficient…"

"Of course, honey. I'll just grab my golf glove and leave you to it."

So Dylan had been right about the golf course. Strange that he'd be taking off so early in the morning on a weekday to hit the green. Then again, politicians were known to hold conferences in some mighty strange places.

Sam ducked into his office and waved the glove as he returned, hesitating at the door. "I tried to call and check on you when I heard about the incident on Sixth Street. What on earth was that about?"

Jana shrugged. "The police aren't sure yet. Sorry I missed your call. I was totally exhausted. I went to bed early."

"Understandable. Remember, you don't have to do this now. Whatever you need, you have friends here ready to step up and help."

"Thanks." Her voice cracked and she snatched a tissue, dabbing at her eyes.

From his position at her side, Dylan noticed she wasn't actually weeping this time.

CHAPTER 3

WHEN SAM'S footsteps faded down the hallway, Jana got up and locked the door again. She'd heard there was an anger stage in the grief cycle and while what currently burned through her veins wasn't precisely related to grief, it felt good to feel something different.

"That bastard." She stalked toward her office but Dylan stepped in front of her. She glared at him.

"Settle down a minute. Bring me up to speed. What did he say that made you so mad?"

"You heard him." She jerked back a step. "I don't have to be in any hurry to *clean out my office*," she said, her anger wobbling a little. She fisted her hands, her mind racing in different directions when she wanted it to stay on the anger. "The governor hasn't so much as hinted about who he'll appoint to fulfill Dad's term. Sam could be out of a job just as well."

"You're hoping you'll be chosen?"

"Hope isn't the right word." Jana considered Dylan's question for a moment. "The appointment isn't impossible. I'm young but I know Dad's values and priorities and I've been a part of Texas politics my whole life."

"No need to borrow trouble then," he suggested. "We'll know when we know. So, are we done here?"

"Not quite." Jana braced her hands on her hips and tried to focus. What was left to do here? She'd gone through her father's office. There wasn't really any need to bother with hers.

"Who is Sam to you—besides being your father's chief of staff?"

Jana shifted her attention back to Dylan. "Sam's been like family my whole life. He's always worked with Dad." She stopped, staring through the doorway at her father's desk as a wave of bitterness washed over her. Someone had cheated her, stolen the most precious person from her life. She would never again stand in this spot waiting for her father to look up from his work and give her that big-as-Texas smile. "Sam's always been direct with me, but he's never been unkind." She faced Dylan again. "Until today. Could that mean something?"

"Probably not what you want it to mean."

His words slowly registered and her stomach knotted up again. She hadn't meant to imply Sam was capable of murder. "No. Not that. Sam loved Dad like a brother." He couldn't be the killer. But someone had to be. Unless she was wrong about everything… she wasn't. Jana refused to believe that. Maybe all she was picking up from Sam was his agreement with Camille and the police. How was it the man who had worked so closely with her father believed he committed suicide?

"Are you reconsidering your theory?" Dylan asked, drawing her from the painful thoughts.

"No. I am not." Her father *had not* killed himself. She knew that in her heart, in her soul. It wasn't the persistent illusion of a heartbroken daughter. Couldn't be. "Let me get the papers. Will you shut down Rose's computer?"

"Sure."

In her office, she started fuming all over again. How could Sam be so certain her services wouldn't be needed by whoever filled her father's senate seat? She knew her dad's vision, his friends and allies, and his agenda for the upcoming session. With her knowledge of issues and the key players on the social policy stage, Jana could be an asset to any appointee. She'd expected a chance to prove it. Implying she'd be booted out was uncalled for.

Tempting as it was to clean out her office and write a heated resignation letter, Claytons didn't give in and they didn't go down without a fight. Growing up in her father's political shadow, she understood the game better than most. It wasn't that she would have any trouble finding another job. The idea that she wouldn't be here to help bring father's plans for the future to fruition weighed on her like an impending failure. The new senator would certainly have his own agenda, but Jana wanted to give her father's wishes a chance, too.

Working to compose herself, she pulled a briefcase and a tote bag from her office closet and returned to her father's desk. Dylan waited in the doorway, watching as she filled both bags to bursting with the paperwork she wanted to examine more closely. Satisfied nothing looked out of place, she turned to him. "Whatever has Sam so convinced I'm out, I hoping golf fixes it. I'll move out if and when the new *senator* asks me to."

Dylan smiled. "That's the spirit." He took the briefcase and the tote from her, his fingers brushing hers and sending a fresh zing of awareness through her system. "By the way, I charge extra for heavy lifting."

"So much for camaraderie," she said, feeling better than she should under the grim circumstances. She couldn't ignore those little tingles that accompanied the most brief and fleeting touch. How foolish and pathetic of her. Who was being unprofessional now?

When she'd locked the office door and they were in alone in the elevator, she thanked him. Not for the tingles, but for being here. Though he was hardly more than a stranger, he kept her from feeling so alone in all this. The few seconds that elapsed before he responded proved incredibly awkward.

"Haven't done much to earn it," he said, hitching a shoulder.

He might not be great at dealing with her tears, but something about him told her there was real compassion lurking behind those intense blue eyes. "You've done plenty." Like saving her life—if that drive-by shooter had been targeting her.

Dylan made one of those male noncommittal sounds, more of a grunt than anything else. "I've done my job."

"Regardless," she turned to him, "you have my gratitude."

He looked away. "It's your dime."

Yes, it was. And she was determined to use it to find a killer and restore her father's reputation. "In that case, let's take all this back to my place and get started wading through the pages over lunch."

His agreement was a curt nod as the elevator doors parted. She accepted more condolences from others headed into the state house. She and Dylan didn't chat on the way to her car. She couldn't think of anything witty and serious topics were best saved until they were alone. Since he'd never returned her car key, she automatically went to the passenger side and waited for him to hit the unlock button. It wasn't worth another argument. She was so distracted with thoughts of what she needed to find to prove her father hadn't killed himself, driving probably wasn't a good idea.

"No protest?" he asked, loading the tote bag and briefcase into the back seat and then opening her door.

"Would it matter?" She slid into the seat. No need for him to know she didn't trust herself to drive just now. She wouldn't have even admitted it to herself yesterday.

"No." A faint smile tilted his lips.

She resisted the wholly feminine response to that expression. As he rounded the hood she shook her head. What was wrong with her this morning? Dylan Parker was here, at her request, in an official capacity. Tingle-inducing sexy or not, he was barely more than a stranger who didn't approve of her roller-coaster emotions. Revealing any sign of attraction would just compound their shaky partnership and make her look completely unstable. If he was uncomfortable with her tears, he would no doubt be ready to run if she turned all needy on him. She couldn't chance driving him away and starting over with another investigator.

Besides, Jana Clayton was not needy. She forced the ridiculous thoughts away and stared straight ahead. He was quiet during the drive. She kept her focus on the road until she couldn't resist any longer. She glanced at his unyielding profile, then at his hands tight on the steering wheel. It was the way he repeatedly checked the mirrors that set off her internal alarm.

"Is something wrong?"

"Not yet." He shot her a smile. "Do you have a particular drive-thru in mind for lunch?"

"I'd rather cook."

"Are you any good at it?" He sent her a questioning look that was just the tiniest bit mischievous.

"Yes. I don't always have time, but when I do I very much enjoy it and I'm damned good at it." Working with her hands would give her time to mull over where they went from here if the loads of papers from her father's office revealed nothing. She opened her mouth to start a discussion along those lines when the car jerked and shifted.

Dylan took his foot off the gas and eased to the shoulder as the unmistakable slap and wobble of a flat tire reverberated through the sedan. A horn sounded and traffic blew by them in fast spurts, matching Jana's racing heart. "Perfect," she muttered, reaching for her cell.

He flipped on the emergency flashers. "Do you have a spare?"

She nodded. "In the trunk, but I can call roadside assistance."

"No need for us to wait. I can take care of it."

"Thanks." She took a deep breath, told herself to relax. Flat tires happened. On the crisis scale this was a minor inconvenience. "Again."

"Wait here," he said. "It won't take me long."

She did exactly as he told her for about twenty seconds and then the incessant *click-click*, *click-click* of the flashers drove her out of the car.

He looked up from fitting the jack to the car's frame. "I needed air," she explained.

He loosened the first lug nut and started on the second. "Still a little ticked at Maguire?"

"A little. Yes." If there was nothing in all those pages, what then? The question would not stop echoing in her head.

With his sleeves rolled back to the elbow and his hands smeared with dirt, Dylan worked effortlessly with the tire iron. The man had a way about him. She could watch him move all day long. Jana considered that she knew basically nothing about him. She glanced at the cars whizzing past. She really shouldn't pry.

"Where's home for you?" she heard herself ask.

"Here and there."

She folded her arms over her middle. "So you get to know everything about me and I know nothing about you? That doesn't seem quite fair."

"Ask whatever you want." He loosened the final lug nut. "I reserve the right to answer as I see fit."

"All right then. Who's waiting for you to be done

56

with this job?" There it was. Only the second question out of her mouth and it was about his relationship status. This was proof positive that she wasn't herself.

"My banker."

"Ha, ha. You must have a personal life."

He eyed the oncoming traffic, then pulled the tire off the car and leaned it against the rear bumper. "What's with the twenty questions?"

"That was one question." *Maybe two.* And a leading statement he'd ignored. "I'm just making conversation," she said, almost convincing herself.

He moved to the trunk and rounded up the spare. "Let's talk about something else."

"Is that the way it works? I don't get to know anything about you?" She was unsure of the protocol for this situation. Clearly he was excessively sensitive about his personal life. Maybe they were more alike than she'd realized. The major difference, the way she saw it, was that her world had an order, an expected action and reaction. Nothing in her life had prepared her for this. For him. "I'm accustomed to schedules and routines and familiarity with those around me."

"This flat could be sabotage," he declared, pointing to a large screw at the edge of the tread of the deflated tire. "A slow leak usually goes unnoticed until you end up with a flat. And let's not forget the drive-by yesterday. There's nothing routine about either event. In fact, at this rate, I think it's safe to say we have a pattern emerging."

"I'm not sure what point you're trying to make." Why was he suddenly so angry?

"Get in the car." He wrestled the spare into place.

He finished the tire change with the speed and finesse of a racecar pit crew, barely giving her time to scoot out of the way as he tossed the flat into the trunk and slammed the lid. She resumed her place in the passenger seat and tried her level best to think of the proper sarcastic remark for when he slid behind the wheel. The man unnerved her on far too many levels.

Once he'd merged with traffic, she tried to explain herself. "I wasn't prying. I'm curious, that's all."

Why not tell him the truth? If this arrangement was going to work, she couldn't hold back. At this point, she felt reasonably confident she could trust him, which was a decent step toward regaining some semblance of control in the world around her. For the past two weeks every little thing had put her on edge, underscoring the sensation that her life was spiraling out of control. Regaining her footing, so to speak, was immensely important.

Dylan shifted in his seat, checking the mirrors. "Do you know anyone on the highway patrol?"

"Of course," she replied, annoyed that he'd once again snubbed her comments. "Why?" She watched him split his attention between the road ahead and whatever was behind them.

"There's about to be an accident."

She watched, stunned, as a black motorcycle pulled out into traffic from the median emergency vehicle access. "Is that the same one as yesterday?"

"We'll see." His hands flexed on the steering wheel.

Jana's fingers wrapped around her fastened seatbelt

as the motorcycle sped by them and then jerked into their lane and hit the brakes. Dylan slowed in response. A second motorcycle roared up to their rear bumper.

"What the hell?"

"Well said." Dylan tapped the brakes again. The bikers adjusted immediately. "Dumb move to pit a bike against a car."

"You have a plan?" She certainly hoped so.

"Make the call, report bikes illegally racing and reckless drivers."

She did as he asked, managing to relay the information to the dispatcher despite the roar of the engines as the motorcycles continued to keep them hemmed in.

"Good job," he said when the call ended.

"Take the next exit," she suggested, her fingers fidgeting with her seatbelt again. They'd have immediate help at the businesses near the off ramp.

"No."

She started to demand why but the bike following them suddenly came up on her side of the car, using the exit lane. The gun was big and ugly, the barrel aimed at her through the window.

Jana screamed.

Dylan slammed on the brakes and pulled the steering wheel hard to the left. Tires squealed and the right rear quarter panel of the car sent one of the motorcycles spinning into the green slope. She wasn't sure if she was praying or cursing as Dylan regained control and squared the car in the lane again.

"Get down!" he ordered as the passenger on the second motorcycle whipped out a weapon.

She ducked, hearing two pops and a sudden whistling of air through the broken windshield.

The car swayed and rocketed forward. Jana held her breath and prayed the highway patrol would hurry. This was it, she realized. This was undeniable evidence that someone really was trying to kill her. Dear God. But why? What did that mean relevant to her father's murder?

Amid the turmoil around her, one thing became frighteningly clear. Her father was right, she could trust no one.

"They're gone," Dylan's voice cut through her panic. "You can sit up now."

She didn't want to. What she wanted to do was curl up into the fetal position until further notice.

"Come on, Jana. Sit up."

This time she obeyed. The windshield looked like something from a movie. Two holes were just to the left of her field of vision. Her stomach lurched. "They tried to kill me."

"Yes," Dylan agreed.

"Pull over." Her stomach roiled. Her heart thundered.

"As soon as it's safe," he said.

"Now. Please. I'm going to be sick." She swallowed the rising tide of terror and bile.

"Go ahead. It's your car."

She scowled at him. "You're being a jerk."

"True." He spared her a brief glance. "But you haven't thrown up yet." He took the next exit and drove past two service stations and a grocery store, parking under the awning of a modest hotel chain. "Let's work at my place this afternoon."

"What about the car?" She swallowed back another wave of nausea. The windshield was a mess, the upholstery was damaged, and there was probably a big dent where he'd collided with that motorcycle. The spare tire was one of those smaller ones that likely had no rubber left on it after Dylan's evasive maneuvers. "And... and the police report?"

"You've done your civic duty and called in the reckless drivers." He pointed at the windshield. "I'll get someone to fix the car. It's not a big deal. You have bigger priorities."

He was so calm. Someone wanted her dead. There was no question now. If Dylan was on the wrong side of the situation, he could've let the shooters succeed. If she'd needed even a smidgen of additional proof she could trust him, she had it now.

Her hands shook and her knees felt like jelly, but she seized the tote bag when he handed it to her. With her purse over her shoulder, she kept her eyes on his back as she followed him through the lobby and up to a room.

Dylan was relieved she hadn't broken down. No tears, no temper, just a blank look in those soft green eyes. He pulled out a chair, urged her to sit down and then handed her a bottle of water from the mini-fridge.

"Thank you." She held the bottle, stared blankly at it.

He'd heard computerized voices exhibit more emotion. "Hey." He opened the water for her. "Look at me, Jana. You're safe." He watched her wide eyes working to focus on his face. "Why don't you take a few minutes?" He pointed to the bathroom. "Grab a shower or something."

"I don't have clean clothes," she said, looking lost. "I don't –"

Her clothing wasn't dirty, but he understood she was badly shaken. "Wash your face, let your hair down." He suddenly wanted to see all that hair tumbling about her face like it had when he'd woken her up this morning. He cleared his throat, banishing that tempting image. "Go on. I'll order lunch."

When she'd closed the bathroom door, he ordered pizza before calling Claudia. While the whiz of the Guardian Agency didn't have any news on yesterday's drive-by, he heard her fingers tapping as she logged today's trouble and arranged for a garage to pick up and repair Jana's car. "I need background on Sam Maguire," he added quietly.

On the other end of the line, the tapping of keys ceased. "Senator Clayton's chief of staff?" Claudia asked.

"That's the one." Dylan glanced at the bathroom door, hoping Jana would take a bit more time. Claudia's fingers rattled over her keyboard again. "How many monitors do you have?"

Another pause was followed by a flurry of typing. "More than you," she said.

"Come on," he teased. "Tell me something about yourself." He'd never met her in person, had no idea about her location. Once he'd signed the paperwork with the Guardian Agency, the attorney who'd hired him gave him a stack of cash, a receipt showing a wire transfer to his bank account, and a cell phone programmed with Claudia's name and number.

"You're incorrigible, Parker."

"I hear all the girls love a bad boy."

Claudia snorted. "You've got a long way to go to be bad enough for me."

He laughed, wondering what it would take to get a face to face with the tech genius who offered long-distance back up on his operations.

"All right," she said. "The car's easy, Parker. I'll send a text when it's back at your location. Taking a deeper look at Maguire will take a few hours."

"What, I'm not your top priority?"

"You will be in thirty-two minutes."

"Precise." He wondered how many other Guardian Agency bodyguards she assisted from wherever the agency had her tucked away.

"Always. Keep an eye on your charge, Parker, the new headlines might upset her."

The line went dead before he could mention the jump drive in his pocket. It would wait. He couldn't upload it with Jana here anyway. Dylan dropped his phone on the desk alongside all the paperwork Jana had pulled from the office. He didn't want to do it, but heeding Claudia's warning, he turned on the television.

A reporter stood in front of the capitol building declaring Senator Clayton an adulterer and insinuating the affair continued despite the intervention of a marriage counselor. Marital strife would sure explain a father's sudden distance from his daughter, Dylan supposed.

"In light of this revelation, Senator Clayton's suicide becomes less shocking," the reporter assessed.

"*Bull.*"

Dylan turned from the television at Jana's outburst. He watched her stroll toward the desk. She'd washed the makeup from her face and changed the tight bun into a loose braid that brushed her shoulders. Tossing her cardigan over the tote, she pulled her white blouse from the waistband of her slacks and unbuttoned the second button from the collar.

The gap only exposed a scalloped edge of lace, but the effect stirred his senses. With an effort, he pulled his mind back to the job. "How much did you hear?"

"Enough to call it what it is." She hit the mute button when the newscaster moved to the next headline. "There is no way he was having an affair."

"What about something new?"

She shook her head. "No way. Before you tell me it explains his reticence and secrecy, I'll remind you of the letter he wrote me."

Dylan flipped off the television. "Anyone can put anything on paper."

"He was faithful in both of his marriages." She shook her head and reached for the tote. "I'm telling you he didn't have time for an affair. Did they even name the other woman or the marriage counselor?"

"No."

"See? Mudslinging. Camille can clear up that nonsense with a short statement."

He wasn't so sure. People scooped up scandal and politics like chips and salsa. "Will she?" Dylan had the basics on Camille, Jana's stepmother, but he didn't know anything about what sort of woman she was. The senator's first wife died when Jana was in seventh grade. Camille, a businesswoman and occasional lobbyist crossed paths with the senator about a year later, but they weren't married until Jana's junior year of high school.

"Assuming we can get her out of bed and in front of a camera," Jana muttered. "If she doesn't say something by tomorrow, I'll ask Sam to put out a statement. First depression and now adultery, these rumors have to stop."

Dylan couldn't see the reason for discrediting a dead man and trying to kill Jana. Who needed to do both? He checked his watch. "Pizza will be here any minute. While we eat, you can tell me what your dad worked on this past year."

When the pizza arrived, he considered it a good sign that she actually ate two slices and downed a cola, but her appetite slowed as she explained more of the senator's work. "Dad's death has to be policy related." She gathered her paper napkin and plate and dumped both in the trash can by the desk. "There are some big votes in the next session," she added, reaching for the briefcase. "There isn't anything else. Still, it seems so wrong that someone would have killed him to change a vote."

"Some kill for less every day," Dylan offered.

Jana laid out the hot topics, and he made notes on his laptop of things he would ask Claudia to double check against the jump drive download from Rose's computer. "I want to see the hate mail," he said, getting up and pacing to the window. "People don't typically go from mad to murder without a few steps in between."

"Have you dealt with many murder cases?"

More than his share. "Enough."

"Before or after you became a bodyguard?"

"Yes."

"Gee, thanks for the insight, Mr. Transparency."

He grinned at her sarcasm. "This isn't about me, it's about you and your dad."

She opened her mouth and snapped it shut again. Returning to the paperwork, she flipped through one stack after another. "Here." She handed him three separate stacks of paper secured with heavy binder clips.

"What's this?"

She took a deep breath. "These were the policy issues Dad and I were most concerned about for the next session. I don't consider any of it worthy of murder."

"If someone wanted your father dead and it wasn't about policy, it had to be personal and now that someone is getting nervous because you're resisting the suicide theory."

Jana frowned. "My murder theory wasn't popular, but I didn't accuse anyone. I didn't even share it with anyone except Camille, Sam and the police. The only way killing me makes sense is if someone doesn't want me filling out the term and voting as Dad would have."

"What if it's both?" If a political and personal vendetta intersected, the suspect pool just got smaller, though he kept that thought to himself. For the most part, she had winnowed the suspect pool to two people with her own assessments. She just hadn't realized it yet.

Seeing two attempts on her life fail, Dylan suspected the next move would likely be an attempt to discredit Jana.

CHAPTER 4

DYLAN THOUGHT his eyes might cross as they read and talked, evaluating and assessing issues and perceived threats. Hours later, after the remaining pizza was demolished all he wanted was a cold beer and a long stretch of silence. When he got the text message that Jana's car had been returned, he jumped at the chance to take her home. They'd both be more comfortable at her place anyway.

In the parking lot, Jana caught him with an exuberant hug when she saw her car looking like new. "How did you do that?"

"I didn't do anything except make a call." He stepped out of her reach for a closer examination of the shallow dent where he'd knocked the biker off the road. "It's not perfect."

"Close enough," she said on a sigh as she walked around the vehicle. "All four tires are new. Even the upholstery's fixed." She opened the door and looked inside at the headrest. "How much do I owe you?"

"We'll figure it out. Get in." He didn't want to give anyone time to take another shot at her.

In the car, he had plenty of the silence he'd wanted, but instead of finding that a comfort, he wondered what twists and turns her mind was taking. By the time he turned into her driveway, he was flat-out worried about her and more than a little surprised his truck was still there and in one piece. Whoever was working against her would have the registration information by now. Soon they'd also be baffled that he didn't have any connection to her.

Let them sweat. He parked Jana's car in her garage and hit the remote to lower the overhead door.

"You don't have to come in," she said, as he reached to pull the tote full of papers out of the back seat.

Maybe he wasn't the only one needing a little distance. "Part of the service." He smiled, but it didn't ease the tension on her face, or the stress in his shoulders. They were making progress, even if he hadn't yet unraveled the plot surrounding her and her father. Their tenuous working relationship seemed to be doing a dance of one step forward and then two back. "I need to make sure the house is clear otherwise you could walk into a trap."

"The security system is on."

"Do I need to give you the stats on how easy it is to beat those?" he asked as they walked in through the garage. She sighed, but kept quiet while he checked windows, doors, rooms and closets.

Finished with the walk-through, he hesitated in the foyer where she waited. "I should stay here tonight."

The two failed attempts on her life wouldn't be the end of whatever was going on.

"No." She said the word firmly, but her face gave away her uncertainty.

"Jana." He thought they'd moved beyond this part.

"I need time alone." She smoothed her hand over her sleek, dark hair. "I don't understand what you do," she said quietly. "Or even how you get it done. It's obvious I can't resolve this without you and I sincerely appreciate your help." She pressed her lips together. "The truth is I need some space before we tackle Dad's study tomorrow."

The admission cost her, he knew that much. The lady took 'independent' and raised it right up to 'control freak'. "All right. I'll be right outside."

Her expression turned contrite. "Do you need a pillow or blankets?"

He shook his head. "I have everything I need."

The urge to grab her and give her a hug had him walking out without saying goodnight. He paused to listen as she locked up and armed the security system behind him.

In his truck, he drove around the block just to throw off anyone who might be watching and then he parked where he had a clear vantage point of Jana's house. He couldn't have the beer he wanted but he could finally get the data from the jump drive to Claudia.

Booting up the rugged notebook computer he kept in the console, he divided his attention between writing his daily report and watching Jana's home. They might not have a lead yet, but he'd learned a lot just by observing a couple of the players. Mainly, he'd learned a lot about the lady he was here to protect. The satisfaction felt nearly as good as the days when he'd been recognized as one of the best deputies in the Montana sheriff's department.

He still wanted to have a look at the hate mail. Just because the senator hadn't taken it seriously when it came in didn't mean it wasn't relevant now. Another thing nagging at Dylan was the prolonged silence out of the second wife. Why didn't Camille, or Maguire for that matter, contradict the marital strife rumors immediately? As Clayton's chief of staff, Maguire had surely gotten a heads up on the so-called newly discovered evidence of unethical behavior.

Jana might be a jumble of twitchy emotions, but today was enough proof for him that the suicide theory was bogus. Dylan's instincts were humming in that familiar 'keep digging' way. She might not want him in the house, but whether she liked it or not, she needed him shadowing her twenty-four-seven until this was resolved.

His cell phone lit up with an incoming text message from Claudia. He read it immediately and his instincts revved again. Sam Maguire had been in Clayton's social circle since high school. Both men had been part of standout football and baseball teams, both attended college at UT-Austin. Through having chosen differing career paths they remained golf and barbeque buddies and Maguire had come on the political scene during Clayton's first campaign.

"Claudia, you're an angel," he muttered, scrolling

through the full report. The men shared an interest in the oil business, but so did most of the old-money families around here. The guy wasn't a saint but Dylan didn't see anything that could be a viable motive.

Damn but Claudia was good. That was the one thing Dylan knew about his employer. He hired only the best. Though Dylan doubted he would ever meet the man who sent the assignments or the paychecks. The anonymity didn't bother him. In fact, it suited him.

He closed down the electronics and went back to his observation of Jana's house. Once Patterson's man arrived, they could work out a rotating watch schedule.

This would be so much easier if she'd let him crash on her couch. He remembered how she'd looked this morning with her chestnut hair spread across her pillow and reconsidered. The truck wasn't easier, wasn't nearly as comfortable, but it was definitely smarter. She was growing more comfortable with him suggesting trust, which was always a good thing. The downside to her growing trust was the questions about his personal life. He didn't discuss his personal life with anyone, not even his family on the rare occasions he made it home for a visit.

Despite his best efforts, his gaze lingered on Jana's bedroom window and his body tightened. The lady needed his help, not his lust. Only once had he been tempted by a woman while on a case. He'd waited to ask her out until after the case was closed and through the courts, but she'd still been his downfall. He'd been in love and she'd been damn good at faking it while working a long con. He'd paid dearly for that mistake. He'd lost the respect of his friends in the department and he'd lost his job. Worse, his dad had passed away three weeks later and Dylan never got the chance to disprove his guilt and to show he was the honorable son his father had raised. That was the wound that festered still.

Dylan was almost relieved when he spotted movement in Jana's backyard. He'd walked the property, knew the motion-activated floodlights should come on any second, but the yard stayed dark. *Nice*. The intruder knew his way around the obstacles, did he? A confrontation gave him a potential outlet for the sharp burst of anger that still accompanied thoughts of his past. He weighed his options and chose the up close and personal route. This had fun written all over it.

With the dome light of his truck turned off, he silently exited the cab and eased the door closed. Whoever was snooping around Jana's house was in for a surprise. He stayed low, skirting the glow of the street lamp as he crept into her backyard. The intruder had definitely tampered with the security system, because the lights that should have come on remained dark.

Using the shadows, Dylan paused and assessed the angles and options. His blood turned cold as he watched the intruder's hesitant movements that went away from the house rather than toward it. The lookout, Dylan decided. The guy in the shadows was keeping watch for someone inside. The team must've approached through the landscaped yards behind Jana's house. Damn it. He should have insisted on staying in the house. Channeling his temper, he waited for the lookout to move away from his position.

Dylan seized the opening and rushed forward, intent on tackling from behind and pinning the lookout to the ground. But the guy turned at the last second. Hands flew up in a rudimentary block even as Dylan took them both down.

They rolled across the soft grass and Dylan clamped a hand over the lookout's mouth, trapping the warning shout. As he fought back, squirming and kicking, Dylan realized too late he was fighting a woman. Well damn.

Nails scraped his arm and came up to do the same to his face. He barely dodged the attack, but she used the momentum to roll him over. He caught her legs between his and twisted until she was under him again. Trapping her wrists above her head with one hand, he kept the other over her mouth, keeping her quiet.

Her breasts heaved under his chest as she struggled for air while she bucked her hips to gain space to use her knees more effectively. He pressed her down with his body, hoping she'd give up soon. A familiar scent, subtle and sweet, he couldn't quite place teased his nose. All her damned squirming was generating an annoying reaction from his body.

"Be still," he growled close to her face. Still wary of the self-defense skills she'd demonstrated, he eased the harsh hold on her mouth just a little to allow her catch a breath. Sure enough, she tried to ram her head into his nose.

"Stop fighting me." He let his full weight sink into

her once more, felt her laboring for breath. "How many are inside?" he growled at her ear.

Her body froze under him and her reply was muffled.

"If you scream," he promised, "I will make you regret it."

She shook her head as much as his grip allowed.

He lifted his hand less than an inch from her mouth, ready to catch the sound if she tried to scream.

"Dylan." She coughed. "Let me up."

Jana. His body processed the recognition faster than his brain. Hearing her say his name that way, a little breathless from the tussle and position, turned him rock hard in an instant. Mad as hell at himself, he scrambled off her. "What the hell are you doing out here?"

"It's my house," she said, sitting up. "I wanted some air."

He ran a hand through his hair. "I saw... I thought you..."

"I get the idea." She waved off his attempt to help her up.

He cleared his throat. "The floodlights should've come on."

"I turned them off so I could have a little peace and, um, watch the stars."

"You should've sent me a text to let me know."

"I'll remember that next time." She turned on her heel and headed into the house. "I don't have my phone with me, but just so we're clear, I'm going inside and straight to bed."

"Good." The images dancing through his head were all too damned good.

"Are you coming?"

An invitation? She couldn't possibly be saying what his body so desperately wanted to hear. Even if she was, he couldn't accept. "What?"

He heard her impatient sigh. "How can you be at your best if you're sleep deprived and tackling random stargazers all night long? I should have thought of that. You can take the guest room."

"You said you didn't want me in your house," he countered. If he followed her in there he wasn't sure he could keep his hands off her. He was fairly confident he could tempt her into something they'd both regret in the morning. But it would be fun as hell tonight.

The solitude of the truck would be as effective as a cold shower. "Set your security system and text me if you need air again." He straightened his shirt. "I'll be in the truck."

Jana watched him stalk away, her body tingling from head to toe. The sensation had nothing to do with the two glasses of wine she'd had or the cool November air. No, this effervescent feeling was all about her *bodyguard*.

The word sent another tremor through her.

She stepped back into her house and pulled the sliding glass door closed. Setting the alarm, she aimed herself deliberately at her bedroom. Oh, the man was dangerous, but not solely in a protective capacity. If she'd been an intruder, she had no doubt how he would've handled the situation. Quick and competent, an intruder would be dead or headed to jail by now.

She could admire his skills, appreciate his dedication, and leave it at that. But here she stood in her bedroom wishing for something completely inappropriate, completely beyond anything she'd ever wished for. She pulled off her t-shirt, catching his enticing masculine scent and she indulged in a moment's fantasy before changing into her nightgown. Dylan's long, hard body had covered hers completely, his warm breath had caressed her cheek. It had been too intimate, once she'd realized it was him sprawled on top of her.

Good grief, she'd nearly kissed him when she'd recognized his voice. She'd told herself the reaction was merely gratitude at the idea that she wasn't about to be raped or murdered. But that was only part of the truth. She'd wanted to kiss him. To feel that arrogant mouth on hers. To know if he tasted as hot as he looked and felt.

She ducked her head under the covers and screamed into her pillow.

She could *not* be attracted to him. *Well, she was only human.* Maybe it was time to cut herself a little slack. The man was sexy and confident. Being attracted was okay, as long as she didn't embarrass herself by acting on it. Short-term flings with strangers had a tendency to grow teeth and bite back during a political career. That's why she'd been so careful, so restricted with her social life. Following in her father's political footsteps was the long-term goal. Every carefully planned step was about getting there, and she couldn't afford to get distracted now.

Dylan was temporary, a professional giving her an assist during a time of need. Growing up, she'd thought she'd find a lasting romance like her parents had shared. The kind of love established in commitment and respect and mutual devotion. So far that man hadn't entered her circle. Gregory Atkins was politically correct, but he didn't incite the affection she remembered between her parents. He hardly incited any response at all. Jana banished the thoughts. Had she always been so focused on education and career that no one who might stir those feelings in her wanted her? She'd always been a good girl, that was true. But even good girls found their happily-ever-afters, didn't they?

Not once had she dreamed of riding off into the sunset with a hot cowboy all too eager for danger. Maybe that was where she'd gone wrong. Jana groaned, aggravated with herself. She threw off the covers and rolled out of bed. Keeping the lights off, she stalked to the bathroom and splashed cool water on her face.

Her father always said a man was only as good as his associates and she needed to keep that in mind. She didn't know anything about Dylan Parker and she knew even less about his associates, beyond an obvious ability to keep her alive. There were far better ways to show her gratitude than lusting after him like he was Mr. Right Now.

She tried thinking of him as a 'valued employee' though the phrase would surely irritate him. Much as she tried to put him in that tidy box, Dylan wouldn't stay there.

She slept fitfully, her dreams peppered with hot, needy visions of a handsome blond cowboy with strong, capable hands and a cocky grin.

But each one of those sweet dreams twisted and ended with her alone, hurt and dying.

CHAPTER 5

FRIDAY, November 16

Having learned the hard way yesterday, Jana woke with her first alarm and was up and ready long before Dylan knocked on her door. Hearing his truck pull into the drive, she opened the door as he came up the walk.

"Morning," he said, touching the brim of his hat.

He wore the same clothes he'd had on last night, but his shirt was wrinkled and untucked and the scruff of his beard burnished his strong jawline. If she judged him by the men she associated with at work every day none of those things would be attractive, but she didn't and they were. Undeniable desire swirled low in her belly.

"Hi. Come on in." She hoped her smile came off as friendly, with no sign of the guilt she felt for having those kinds of thoughts. It wasn't easy facing the man who'd starred in her fantasies all night long. "I was about to start breakfast."

She tried not to fidget as Dylan filled her foyer, quietly looking her over from head to toe. Other than a few sore muscles and a bruise on her hip that didn't even show yet, she was fine. Knowing she'd landed a couple of decent blocks, she was tempted to ask how he was feeling. She'd at least had the benefit of a comfortable bed.

"Breakfast sounds great." He shrugged off the backpack he'd looped over one shoulder. "I was hoping I could clean up first."

"Sure." Just what her imagination needed, more fodder. "Second door on the—"

"Left," he finished. "I remember."

Of course he remembered. His line of work demanded an eye for details. She walked back to the kitchen resisting the urge to run. They were adults, capable of putting last night's innocent mistake behind them. "Employee," she reminded herself hearing the sound of water in the hall bath.

She wasn't sure which was worse, imagining him under the shower spray, or watching him stroll into her kitchen a few minutes later with damp hair and a freshly-shaved face. His white button down shirt was open at the collar, and the dark jeans, black belt and boots completed the polished appearance. "Eggs?" she managed, recovering from a suddenly-dry mouth.

"Please." He circled around the table toward the coffee pot. "You didn't have to cook." He helped himself to a coffee mug, filling it to the brim while he watched her serve.

"It relaxes me," she admitted.

"Lucky me." He brought his coffee to the table and sat down across from her.

"Did you sleep okay?" Small talk felt like the polite thing to do.

"Here and there." He took a bite of the eggs and his eyelids drifted closed. "Wow. You need to relax more often."

She felt heat creeping into her cheeks at his heartfelt praise. "I'm glad you approve." It felt so domestic sharing a meal and watching him wake up with coffee and food she'd prepared. Slathering jam across a biscuit, she cut her wistful fantasy short. Almost in time.

As a senator's daughter her entire life, she'd grown up under the microscope of society columns and social censure. Her relationships had been as thoughtfully cultivated as her education and extra-curricular activities. The only difference was, none of the relationships had ever panned out. Not even the one she had hoped would, primarily because her father had wanted so desperately to see her happy. But Gregory had been wrong for her. She was very grateful she had recognized the mistake before taking that irrevocable step.

She watched Dylan devour his breakfast. It wouldn't be long before someone discovered she had a new man hovering near the house, accompanying her to the office. The rumors would be tough to overcome if the college story was challenged.

When she'd reached dating age, her father and stepmother had aimed her at intelligent, successful businessmen who understood the balance of perks and sacrifice involved with a political career. But no one stirred her senses like Dylan. Maybe it was the bad-boy edge or simply the bizarre circumstances of their association. As unkind as it made her feel, she recognized that to some degree her reaction to him was about distraction. Whatever drew her to him, it didn't matter. He wasn't a candidate for romance and she wasn't doing herself any favors daydreaming about the impossible.

She reached for the coffee carafe and filled Dylan's coffee mug. "When we're at the house, I'd like to take some time with Camille."

"You two are close?"

Jana nodded as she poured cream into her coffee.

"No wicked stepmother tales?"

"It took me a while to come around," she admitted, remembering those early challenges. "I was just entering high school, prone to angst and drama, and missing my mom."

"Understandable."

"To a point." She couldn't quite meet his gaze. "I was a brat and I didn't want to share my dad. Camille was patient." Jana sipped her coffee. "They both were. Camille eventually got it through my head that she wasn't trying to replace my mom. She wanted to be a friend and confidant. We've been close ever since."

"That's good I guess."

She shook her head. "No guessing required. She and my dad were an excellent team. His death has left her reeling."

"I haven't checked the news this morning. Did she clear up the affair rumor?"

Jana shook her head. "I'll mention it to her. She may

not have heard anything since she's completely shut herself off from the world." She watched Dylan closely when he didn't reply. "What are you thinking?"

He held up his hands. "It's standard investigative practice to look at the spouse first in situations like this."

"No one but you and I are looking at this situation as a murder. But it doesn't matter." Jana stood, taking the dishes to the sink. "She's not a killer. She loved my father."

"Good to know." He followed her and gently nudged her away from the sink. "You cooked, I'll clean."

"That's silly. Finish your coffee."

He shrugged. "We'll have to disagree on that."

She gave in gracefully, in the interest of self-preservation. When he was close, close enough for her to catch the whiff of soap on his skin and feel the warmth of his body, she wanted to get closer. "However we find Camille," she said as she moved back to the table, "the goal is sifting through Dad's study." She gave herself points when her voice didn't crack with emotion.

He shot her a long look. "You sure you'll be okay?"

She nodded. "I'll have to be."

"If it's too much, I can take care of the search while you visit with Camille."

She appreciated the offer, knowing she'd given him good reason for the concern. "I want to do this." Thinking of her stepmother, she added, "If it comes up, we'll give Camille the university library line."

"Got it." He set the clean skillet aside to air dry. "Any

physical evidence of the murder is likely gone at this point. What do you hope to find?"

"I'm certain you're right about that," she agreed. "As soon as the police released the scene, Camille had a cleaning and restoration service come in and take care of… things. She refused to leave the room until they were finished. She oversaw every step."

She tried to stop the scene from playing out in her mind, but it was no use. Thankfully the suicide scenario never happened, not even in her head, it was always someone pointing a gun at her father. Someone she couldn't see.

Shaking off the ugly images, she went on, "The hate mail since we didn't find it at the office." She caught the surprise as his eyebrows arched. "Dad kept work confined to the study when he did bring it home. I can get the bank records if we need them. I'll nudge Camille about fending off those rumors." It sounded logical and gave her a reasonable plan of action, and, she told herself, she would be fine. Logic and reason would prevail.

Several minutes later, as he backed his truck out of her driveway, she realized he had warned her not to let her emotions rule her. "That first day," she confessed, "you were right."

One eyebrow dipped low over his eye. "About?"

"I've let my emotions twist me up," she said. "I've been operating solely on emotion, letting grief dictate my theory."

"You lost your dad," he said. "That isn't easy to cope

with under normal circumstances. Your fear that his death was a homicide makes it even harder."

While she appreciated his understanding, she had to hold firm or she'd never get through this. "Still, I need to think clearly. It's one of the things I was contemplating last night before you... arrived."

"Arrived," he echoed, clearing his throat. "That's one way to put it." He stretched his arm across the seat and tapped her shoulder. "I should've asked earlier. Did I hurt you?"

"No," she replied, smothering a smile that made her feel completely foolish. He was being courteous and she couldn't read more into it than that. "I should've thanked you last night."

"For?"

"Doing your job, even if you were protecting me from myself." She considered it a great accomplishment when he laughed. While they'd probably never be real friends, it felt like they were finally on good working terms. "I've never told anyone how much I enjoy being alone in the dark."

"Why not?"

"The night became the one place where everyone's expectations disappeared. I could dream anything, be anyone. Fail at math, excel at dance. Anything's possible under the stars with no one watching."

"Who did you want to be?"

"Myself," she said. Yet here she was on the verge of thirty and she hadn't figured out how to make that happen. She had always been Senator Clayton's daughter.

For the first time in her life the thought made her truly sad. Her father was gone. Who was she supposed to be now?

Dylan drove out to her childhood home without any directional assistance from her, reminding her again just how comprehensive his case file was. Rather than dwell on questions he'd never answer, she brought up the three studies they'd reviewed yesterday. Neither of them could draw a viable connection to anyone with enough desperation, means, or access to kill her father.

"Maybe Camille will have some insight," she said. "Dad might've told her something she doesn't realize is related."

DYLAN SHIFTED in the driver's seat, keeping an eye out for the next turn. Sharing details with Camille felt like a mistake, especially if the woman wasn't coping well with being widowed. But Jana would want more than his gut instinct to back up his opinion. "Have you told her you think the suicide was staged?"

"Not in so many words. I mean…"

He expected waterworks any second now, but when he slid a glance her way, her expression was resolute.

"When she told me he was dead—"

"Wait. You heard it from *her* first?"

"Yes." Jana took a deep breath. "I came out immediately and helped with the final arrangements. I didn't make any secret about my disbelief that he'd killed himself. It just wasn't possible."

"No one agreed with you."

"Not even Camille. Like you, she chalked up my reaction to shock and grief. I never mentioned it to her again, but maybe today is a better time."

As he slowed down for the last turn into the long tree lined drive, Dylan hoped Jana was right.

"She is so lost without him," Jana murmured.

"That surprises you?"

"A little," she confessed. "They were in love, but she kept a full schedule between her career and other interests. Incorrectly, I assumed that meant they weren't as close as he'd been with Mom. They'd only been married twelve years, together for thirteen, but she's a wreck."

Based on his professional and personal experience he'd learned that duration had little to do with the impact when a relationship ended, especially if someone was keeping secrets. "Let's wait and see how she's feeling," Dylan offered. While he believed Jana was right about murder, he didn't want to increase the odds against them before they could pinpoint the responsible person.

The spouse was always a suspect, whether Jana wanted to see it that way or not.

Tall, iron gates crowned with a 'C' parted as they approached. "I sent a text," Jana explained as he proceeded up the driveway. The house sprawled out from a circular drive. "Just park here in front."

The housekeeper, Helen, greeted them at the front door. Jana introduced him as her friend from college and the woman welcomed Dylan with a big smile.

"How's Camille today?" Jana asked as they were led into the kitchen for coffee.

"Better." Helen poured two cups from the carafe on the counter. "She went to the boutique this morning."

Dylan figured the boutique was one of Camille's business interests. According to the file, she had extensive assets of her own, including a number of businesses. He surveyed the modern appliances and sleek stone countertops of the enormous kitchen. If Camille benefitted from any life insurance, she wouldn't need to apply it to a kitchen remodel.

"Well, I'm glad she's getting back to her routine," Jana was saying. "The university library wants to put together a section on Dad's accomplishments. Dylan and I have pulled a few things from the office, but I know there's more they'll want from the study."

"Oh, you can't do that," Helen said, her voice rising.

"Why not?"

"It would upset her." Helen laid a hand over her heart. "She can't bear anything out of place. No one is allowed in there."

"In Dad's study?" Jana frowned.

Helen nodded. "She saw me dusting and told me never to go in there again."

"That's unreasonable," Jana argued.

Helen patted Jana's cheek. "You're young. You don't understand how she misses him. She spends hours in there every day."

"Doing what?" Dylan asked when Jana seemed speechless.

"Sitting and staring from what I can tell." Helen

turned a worried gaze to Jana. "I think you should spend more time here. There's too much empty space for her right now. She's not herself at all."

"I'll speak to her," Jana promised.

Dylan knew Jana's promise was sincere but he was more curious about the crease between her eyebrows. He'd quickly learned that meant she wasn't pleased with what she'd heard or seen. He'd noticed it right before she lost her temper over Maguire's comments.

"For now Dylan and I will only take a quick peek. She'll never know we were there."

"If you insist." Helen shrugged. "Don't blame me if she gets upset."

Dylan pushed back from the counter. "The university means no disrespect to the family. Senator Clayton is an inspiration. What we have planned to honor his legacy will take some time if we're going to do it right."

The tension eased from Helen's shoulders. "I'm glad to hear the university will do the right thing. Maybe she won't be so upset."

"We try." He tapped his cup. "Thank you for the excellent coffee."

They left Helen beaming in the kitchen as they headed to the study. "Is your house the Versailles of Texas?" he whispered for Jana's ears only.

She giggled and that silly, girlish sound inexplicably moved him.

He brushed it off and stared up at the soaring coffered ceiling. The place felt more like a museum than a home. There were seating areas and artwork on display. The floors were marble and wood, all gleaming like brand new. The dining room looked bigger than his apartment, with a table that could seat twenty with ease.

"You get used to it."

"Did you really grow up here?"

She made another of those tinkling sounds. "Dad and Camille did extensive remodeling a few years ago, but yes, it was always really big. This part of the house is perpetually set for entertaining."

Entertaining heads of state. Of course, he ran in a different social stratosphere than Texas politicians. "The last time I saw a table that big it was outdoors."

"Where?"

"On a ranch in Montana," he replied without thinking. "It was big enough for the family and the ranch hands. Aren't you an only child?"

She shot him a look. "You know I am."

"It's a lot to take in," he admitted, feeling like his head was on a swivel. It gave him new insight on the woman at his side.

"I should've brought you through the back if you think this is so special." She turned down a wide hallway.

"Why didn't you?"

"I was afraid you'd develop grill envy," she teased, grinning up at him as she made another turn.

The expression transformed everything about her face and he nearly tripped over his feet. "What?"

She opened the French doors to the study. "We do things big in Texas. There's a courtyard right through that door." She pointed directly across the room. "Next to that is an outdoor kitchen, the star of which is a massive grill."

He looked around the well-appointed room. Not a single sign that the senator had died here remained. The cleaning and restoration was impeccable. He crossed to the exterior door, but he'd already forgotten the grill. "So there's direct access. Someone here to see your dad doesn't have to come through the formal part of the house."

"It's a privilege he granted judiciously."

"Always good to remind people who's got the power," Dylan agreed. Clayton had power and influence to spare and according to all accounts he wielded both with care and thought. Who, in his inner circle, resented that power and influence enough to kill him?

As Jana booted up Clayton's computer, Dylan did a physical search starting at the exterior door. He noted the security system contacts, but again, it would've been easy enough to bypass them as an owner or as an intruder.

Jana managed this search with more composure and less chaos. Likely out of courtesy for Camille as well as her father. Relieved as he was, he couldn't help commenting as he searched the credenza behind the desk. "You're remarkably calm."

"It surprises me, too." Her gaze drifted around the room. "You know, I haven't sat in this chair since I was ten or twelve."

"Forbidden territory?"

"No. Dad wasn't like that. It was more like respect for the 'seat of power'," she said, adding air quotes and a deep voice for effect. "As I started to understand what he did, it didn't feel like a game to play senator anymore. When Camille had the house redone, this was one of the first rooms to be gutted. It wasn't the same after that. I guess all those little girl games and fantasies went out with the old furnishings and book-shelves."

"Why do you think she comes in here every day?" He wasn't buying the housekeeper's explanation. He scoured the numerous bookshelves for any clue to the step-mother's motives.

Jana inhaled. "Maybe because this was where he took his final breath. Before... it always smelled like him. I suppose the cleaning agents took that away."

Dylan figured that was as good a theory as any, but he wondered if Camille was looking for something like they were. While Jana went through the desk and the credenza, he examined books, admired framed pictures, art work, and a star-shaped sculpture until his fingers landed on something that didn't feel right on the spine of a book. Pulling it from the shelf, he opened it and found a hiding place. Half a dozen letters, all addressed to the senator were tucked inside.

"I think this volume could be nice, if your step-mother can part with it."

Jana swiveled the chair and looked at the book he held open for her. She opened the first of the letters. Her hand went to her chest. "No wonder I didn't find a hate mail file. He had it hidden away."

The security system panel on the wall chimed.

"That's someone coming through the front gates,"

Jana explained, still rifling through the letters. "Camille may be back."

Dylan assumed as much. "Maybe we should put that away and have a look at it later."

"Good idea." She placed the book into her oversized purse while he adjusted the shelves to cover its absence.

Another chime sounded. Jana looked up. "That was the front door."

They worked swiftly to ensure all was as they'd found it when they entered the study.

"This room is so quiet," he said. "You wouldn't know that company had arrived without the security system alerts."

"We had it soundproofed last year so J.D. could concentrate," a smooth, feminine voice replied from the doorway.

He and Jana were caught. Camille looked docile in a dove gray suit, but there was an annoyed edge to her expression. "What are you doing in here?"

Jana's smile faltered and she came out of the chair as if it had zapped her. "We're choosing a few things for the new section honoring Dad at the university library." She wrapped Camille in a gentle hug. "How are you? You look wonderful."

"Thank you," she said, looking past Jana. "I didn't see any request from the university." Her eyes raked Dylan from head to toe.

Jana made the introductions quickly, adding, "As an old friend, Dylan came directly to me."

"I see."

Her tone suggested she didn't see at all. Dylan

stepped forward, breaking the awkward moment. "I've heard a lot about you, Mrs. Clayton," he said, extending his hand. "It's a pleasure."

"Dylan?" Camille's gaze shifted between them. "I don't recall Jana mentioning your name."

"College was ages ago," he said. "I'm sorry for your loss, Mrs. Clayton."

She acknowledged that with a regal dip of her head. "I'm glad Jana has a good… friend available during this difficult time." Camille pressed her fingers to her lips. "Forgive me. I'm an absolute wreck."

Her eyes filled, but the tears didn't fall. If the step-mother was a wreck, his instincts were failing him. He recognized the cold edge under the polished exterior of this elegantly grieving widow. He'd seen it occasionally during his law enforcement days in Montana. While he should be grateful he'd only missed that dangerous verge once, the incident that ended his career had made him a more cautious man.

For a split second he experienced a burst of gratitude for that mistake. Otherwise he wouldn't be here to help Jana. Whether she realized it or not, she definitely needed someone on her side. He was suddenly and inexplicably glad it was him.

"Sit down," Jana suggested to Camille. "The university has the best intentions." She pulled the guest chair closer to her stepmother. "You'll like it."

Dylan stood next to Jana, hands in his pockets, not daring to sit in Clayton's chair or lean against the desk.

"It's just so fast." Camille blotted her eyes with a tissue. "I'm not ready to part with anything."

Jana held one of Camille's hands between both of hers. "That's not what the university is asking," she said. "We're sharing what made Dad so special. Dylan explained to me how honoring Dad will inspire others to follow his example. Anything displayed there will be expertly cared for."

"His legacy of generosity and service will live on," Dylan added. "We'll display only copies if that's easier on you."

"You don't look like a librarian," Camille said, her gaze sharp, despite the smile on her lips.

"Thanks." He bobbed his head. "I make every effort to destroy the stereotype."

"I really feel this is for the best," Jana urged. "It gives us something positive to work on."

Camille's gaze drifted around the room, but Dylan wasn't buying the wounded expression on her face. "I went to the boutique this morning to silence those wagging tongues."

"Have you made a statement to the press?"

"Nothing so formal." Camille laced her fingers together in her lap. "I won't dignify those nasty rumors about affairs and marital counseling with a statement."

"Do you want me to clear things up on your behalf?"

"Who would believe you?" Camille snapped, then turned instantly repentant. "I'm sorry. Oh, sweetheart, I'm just so irritated by that nonsense. Your offer is thoughtful, but would it really change anything? You know those vultures in the media. They've circled us for years and now they're closing in."

"It can't hurt to try," Jana said brightly, patting her

stepmother's hand. "I'll talk with Sam. We'll draft something and run it by you this afternoon. I'm sure he's already looking into it."

"Probably so." Camille sighed and pushed to her feet. "I need to lie down."

"Okay," Jana said. "We won't be long. Take care of yourself."

Camille paused at the door, motioning them to join her. "Leave the library acquisitions for another day. I just cannot cope with anyone—not even you, dear heart —touching his things right now."

"But Father," Jana started to argue.

"Of course, Mrs. Clayton." Dylan cut her off. He scooped Jana's purse from the floor and handed it to her. Better to let the woman think she was fooling them. "There's no rush at all."

"Thank you for understanding." With Dylan and Jana in the hallway, Camille pulled the doors shut behind her.

Exchanging quick farewells, Dylan noticed Camille only headed for the family side of the house once he and Jana were under Helen's escort back to the front door.

Just what was the lady hiding?

CHAPTER 6

JANA COULDN'T SHAKE the uneasiness crawling under her skin. She'd never been treated as an outsider in her childhood home. Helen had hovered and Camille was definitely in an odd mood. Her stepmother's eyes had been clear despite the display of tears, the clouds of sorrow gone. Her voice held a sharp edge Jana hadn't heard before. When she'd hugged Camille, the perfume was all wrong for a trip to the boutique. Jana knew her stepmother's routine far too well.

Then again, maybe Jana was grasping at straws? Giving herself a mental shake to dispel her increasing paranoia, she turned to Dylan as he drove away from the house. "Was that weird, or was it just me?"

"Which part?"

"Camille." *Although Helen had been off too.* "That's how I always thought it would be," she said absently.

He drummed his fingertips on the steering wheel. "What do you mean?"

She looked at her purse on the floorboard and

thought of the hollowed out book of hate mail along with the strange files on her dad's computer. Too bad reading in the car made her queasy or she'd be digging in right this instant.

"When Camille first came into the picture I had the normal wicked stepmother worries, certain I'd be sent away, pushed out of Dad's life. But it wasn't like that."

"So the type of conversation the two of you just had isn't normal?"

"Not even close." According to the will, the house belonged to Camille, but Jana was starting to wonder if she needed to claim the artwork and sentimental things her father had earmarked for her before her stepmother changed the locks. *Or worse.*

"Death brings out the abnormal side of people," he said. "I noticed you didn't cry while we were there."

"No, I didn't."

"Abnormal," he said, taking his eyes off the road long enough to emphasize his point.

"Are you trying to be insensitive?"

"Maybe," he agreed. "Humor me. I expected the visit to your father's study to be harder on you. What changed?"

Confusion twisted her thoughts. "I'm not sure." Wouldn't it be nice if she'd run out of tears? "I went in there expecting to be the rock for my stepmother."

"Because Camille is so devastated?"

"Yes." Her stepmother had looked pretty good today, but a trip to the boutique would require her best presentation, no surprise there. What did surprise her was that if she'd gone to the boutique, why had she suddenly returned to the house? More importantly, why wasn't she wearing her signature *Camille* scent?

"You do a pretty impression of a rock," he observed.

"Is that a compliment?"

He nodded and shot her a grin. "It is. Don't get used to it. I give them sparingly."

She wasn't sure how to react to his admission. Jana felt more secure sticking with the case. "Camille mentioned visiting the boutique, but I'm not so sure. How long do you think we were there before Camille caught us?"

"Half an hour maybe. What are you thinking?"

"I think Helen called Camille. The drive times would've been right, but I don't think Camille was at the boutique."

"Because," Dylan prompted.

She hesitated, bracing for his skepticism. "She didn't smell right."

"Go on."

Jana couldn't believe he wasn't laughing at her. "You believe me?"

"Let's say I'm open to a full explanation," he clarified.

"During the holiday season, Camille uses a spicy fragrance in the boutique. She claims it puts people in a buying mood and it's named after her. She had it created in France exclusively for her. She has others, but she always wears that one in November and December. Always."

"All I caught was a thick cloud of flowers when she walked in."

"Exactly. No cinnamon apple, no sugar cookie, just

lots of perfume. She likes standing out from all the other holiday scents."

"You're thinking about the rumors."

"I am," she admitted, her chest heavy with the idea. "It's a big leap. Huge. But what if she was the one having an affair? I thought she and Dad were happy together. There's never been a whiff of impropriety." What if she'd been wrong? The idea hurt more than she wanted to articulate just now. The idea that her father might have been betrayed by the woman he loved was unthinkable.

"It's hard to shift an opinion of someone you care about without strong evidence," Dylan said. "Sometimes it's tough even with plenty of evidence."

"Is that the voice of experience talking?" Jana turned to him. Was a bad experience why Dylan Parker didn't like answering personal questions?

He raked his fingers through his hair. "Let's get back to the perfume."

For reasons she refused to dwell on, she wanted him to open up. Would that be a mistake for both of them? Uncovering the truth about her father's death was too important to risk mistakes. Still, she thought she wanted to know more. She might like the man under the bodyguard-investigator hat.

Setting aside the foolish musings, she concentrated on what she knew about her stepmother's methodology. "Camille uses every tool she has. Brains, clothing, fragrance, connections. She brings out whatever the situation needs and applies liberally to get what she wants. She's quite wealthy in her own right. *If* something is going on with her and she's somehow involved in this, it won't be about money."

"Is that how she landed your dad?"

Jana instantly regretted the way she had framed Camille. "She isn't cold or as mercenary as I made it sound. She has her business side and is tough as nails in that arena, that's what I meant."

"Whichever side she was showing, she wasn't giving off warm fuzzies back there."

"We were in a space she considers hers." The defense was automatic, but Dylan had a point. Jana had to stop evaluating people based on the past, but it was difficult to imagine someone you loved was capable of something as terrible as murder or even conspiracy of some sort. Be that as it may, she had been in politics long enough to know people were not always what they seemed.

"*Uh-huh.*" Dylan cleared his throat. "If it wasn't suicide, then the killer is someone he knew well."

And by default, someone *Camille* knew well. "I understand what you're saying, but where's her motive?" There was only so much Jana could process without losing her grip on the composure she'd managed so far today. "The perfume she was wearing is one she uses when meeting with powerful men."

"Smart. I'll bet she slips right under the defenses of the boy's club."

"She learned to capitalize on being underestimated. If you're implying she uses sex to get what she wants, you'd be wrong."

He flared his hands in surrender. "I'm sure she's terrific when she isn't grieving."

"Lots of Dad's friends and associates earned direct access through the study door when he was home," Jana said. She couldn't let him fixate on Camille. There had to be other, more logical suspects. She couldn't believe Camille was capable of murder.

"Did Camille tell you all her secrets?"

Jana shook off the worry. "What do you mean?"

"How do you know what she used her various fragrances for?"

"She was the mother figure in my life." She shrugged. "More importantly, I wanted my father's respect and admiration when it came to my career, so I suppose I studied Camille since she had earned both."

"My sister did the same. She turned into our mother as she got older." The hint of a smile tugged at his lips. "She disciplines her kids the same way Mom did us. Her Christmas dressing is the same recipe."

"Do you visit your family often?" His entire demeanor changed when he spoke of his family. The alertness softened around his eyes and mouth.

"I was glad your gate code worked," he said, his voice edging toward stern again. "Do you have keys and a personal code for the alarm system?"

"Sure. Why does it matter?" She decided not to bother mentioning that he'd ignored her question. He was controlling the conversation, steering it away from him for a reason she suspected wasn't all about her being a client.

"In case we need to go back in undetected."

Jana realized he was thinking about something else entirely. "You thought she might have changed the codes."

Stopped for a traffic light, he leaned across the cab of the truck. "I've met her once," he said. "You've known her for years. My job, in addition to protecting you, is to find the truth. If you didn't shoot your father—if not Sam or Camille or Helen—who did?"

The bald truth stung, but even her father had warned her not to trust anyone. "You're right." Dylan didn't have anything to gain beyond a paycheck. That was the whole reason she'd looked for an objective third party and yet here she sat on the defensive, finding reasons for everyone to be innocent.

Fisting her hands on her thighs, she resisted the urge to dig into the hate mail. It might be better, more expedient, for him to review it first. "Can you drop me at the state house, please? There are some things I want to look into while you're going through the hate mail."

"In case you forgot about last night already, I'm not letting you out of my sight. We'll go to the office together."

Of course he had to remind her of last night. Hopefully the tidal wave of sensations accompanying the memory, like the heat swirling in her belly and the restless feeling a little lower, weren't obvious to him. "I'm safe at the capitol," she said. "Security is everywhere."

"Yet you didn't ask them to help you with this."

He had her there. "Okay, but what will you do while I'm working?"

"I'll be working too. There's enough space in your

office for both of us. I'll go through the hate mail, like you suggested."

She disagreed with the assessment that there was plenty of room. It had been tough enough working in the close confines of his hotel room yesterday. After their wrestling match in the dark, after feeling the strength of him stretched out over her body and the lusty dreams…

"Jana?"

She snapped out of it, feeling the heat flooding her face. "My mind wandered. Sorry."

"*Uh-huh.*"

She had the distinct impression he knew exactly where her mind had wandered. "What did I miss?"

He shot her another grin. "An opportunity to argue with me about my protective services."

"That'll teach me to allow my mind to wander." Especially along that path.

He turned onto North Congress Street and entered the parking garage. When he'd pulled into a visitor's space, he cut the engine and turned her way. "The sooner we clear this up, the sooner you won't be stuck with me following you around."

"Right." *Sensible.* That was exactly what she wanted. He'd rounded the hood and opened her door before she could open it herself. "Thanks." She hesitated before getting out, enjoying the eye to eye view.

His blue eyes were so bright and steady, his unflinching gaze exuding confidence in himself and his abilities. "How did you wind up here?" she asked, knowing he likely wouldn't answer this personal question any more than he had the others.

"You mean working as a protector with the Guardian Agency?

She nodded.

"Long story." He stepped back, giving her more room to hop out of the truck. "If you still want to know when we've resolved your situation, I'll tell you."

"I'll want to know," she promised as they started up the long walk. "I'd even take a quick preview now, if you don't mind."

He laughed, the low, rusty sound intriguing her. "Things went south in Montana, so I went south, too."

"Oh, how informative."

He opened the door for her. "You asked for a preview. Even blockbuster movies only give you a teaser."

It scared her to realize how much she wanted the entire feature. Was she latching onto the one person who listened to her murder theory? Or was she fascinated by Dylan because something about him cranked up her hormones? Neither option was typical behavior for her. Was the loss of her father causing her to take risks she normally wouldn't have?

Whatever the reason, she liked this man. He could be brutally straightforward, but he'd done his job—more than she realized she'd hired him to do—and saved her life twice. When she wasn't on the verge of tears, he listened attentively. All of that made her think there were several more layers to Dylan Parker than the one she noticed that first day.

As they cleared security and found themselves alone in the elevator she asked, "You left Montana because of a woman didn't you?"

His eyes were full of lethal charm whenever he smiled, but the scowl on his face now was intimidating. Blond eyebrows dipped low over eyes that were cold and hard. She'd crossed a line, obviously, but while that gaze told her to back off, she realized she wasn't the least bit afraid. "Forget I asked."

DYLAN KNEW he wouldn't forget, primarily because he wanted to tell her the whole story. Dumb, but true. Maybe if he made it relevant to her situation she'd be more willing to look at the people she knew as potential suspects.

"You can be pushy," he said as the elevator doors opened.

Instead of being insulted, she aimed a grin at him. "That's a big compliment in the political arena."

Something had shifted since Maguire had ticked her off and the bikers had taken another shot at her. Her stepmother's behavior this morning had an impact as well. He liked this edge of determination. Even if she wasn't quite ready to start pointing fingers, she was distancing herself from the emotions and getting closer to thinking objectively.

As they returned to the senator's office suite, she introduced him to Rose, the receptionist, and after a few pleasantries, they retreated to Jana's office.

Dylan had brought in his computer bag from the truck and between the update he hoped Claudia had sent and the book of hate mail, he had more than enough to keep him busy while she took care of whatever was on her mind.

She cleared a small worktable for him in the corner near the window. Though she apologized for the lack of space, he considered the position an advantage. Anyone who walked in to speak with her wouldn't see him right away. A few unguarded seconds often proved informative in cases like this.

While his computer booted up, he started with the hate mail, figuring it would be easy to hide his search by just closing the book. It didn't take long to realize why Clayton had kept the handwritten letters spouting fury, outrageous accusations, withdrawal of support, and worse. For a popular guy, he had plenty of people willing to vote against him, but none of the letters looked recent.

At her desk, Jana worked in studious silence until Rose popped in and asked about lunch. While the receptionist handled the deli run, Dylan used the time to examine the senator's office again. Based on his observations of Clayton's study and without any fear of offending Jana, he made quick work of his second time through the bookshelves. He found another hollowed out book, this one empty, but he also noticed a familiar sculpture.

Checking the pictures on his phone, he realized the two stars were identical. It had to be significant. He picked up the small piece and examined it closely. A panel on the base popped loose and he discovered an odd shaped key.

He was about to go share the news with Jana when he heard Maguire's voice in the outer office. Pocketing the key, he pulled one of the senator's philosophy books off the shelf and eased himself into one of the visitor's chairs in front of the big executive desk.

"Glad I caught you," Maguire was saying. "I just came from a meeting with the governor."

"Has he decided who will finish Dad's term?"

Dylan hoped Jana, or someone smart enough to keep her around, would be chosen. Much as he ignored politics, spending time with her was giving him a view of the positive, effective side of the things.

"With only a year left, the governor went with the obvious choice."

"Really?" Jana's voice brightened with anticipation.

"Oh, not me," Maguire said. "Though I would've been honored."

What a jerk, Dylan thought. The man had to know Jana considered herself the 'obvious choice.' He leaned a bit toward the door, hoping to catch a peek at Maguire. Sure enough, the chief of staff stood tall, his chest puffed out, looking as smug as he sounded. Dylan had been involved in nasty cases, done some things that would make most people cringe, but few things turned ugly as quickly as money and politics.

Holding the book, Dylan stood up and stepped into Maguire's view. "Did you come to tell Jana the job's hers?"

Maguire might've given himself whiplash as his head swiveled toward Dylan. "What are you doing here?"

He held up the book. "The university library. According to my notes, Senator Clayton enjoyed philosophy."

"Yes, he did." Maguire nodded, but the tension showed on his face.

"The job is Jana's?" Dylan stepped up next to Maguire. "That's great. We'll have to celebrate tonight."

"No." Maguire said sharply. "The governor felt the stress would be too much for her." He gave Jana a smile that looked more like a sneer. "Camille will serve the final year of the term."

"Oh. That's wonderful news," Jana said, sounding sincere. "I'll want to be there for the swearing in."

"Of course." Whatever else was on his mind, Maguire clearly didn't want to discuss it in front of Dylan. "You'll want to clear anything you remove for the library with Mrs. Clayton."

"Don't worry about that, Sam." Jana flicked her pencil between her fingers, the first sign of impatience Dylan had noticed. "We aren't removing anything Camille will need."

With a sober nod, Maguire turned for his office on the other side of the reception area.

Dylan couldn't resist the opportunity to test Maguire's reactions. "Other than a few old books, we're making copies of the important documents." Ignoring Jana's gasp, he focused on the way Maguire nearly tripped over his feet. "I have to agree with Jana that it's less awkward to do it now. We'll be done and out of the way long before the new senator—Mrs. Clayton—needs the office."

"That's, ah, quite considerate," Maguire said, closing his office door.

Dylan strolled into Jana's office, ready to show her the key, but stopped short at the furious look blazing in her eyes.

All but leaping out of her chair, she cornered him at the work table. "What was that about?"

He held his ground. "Baiting the bear?" He shrugged. "The guy bugs me. Besides, he started it with that 'obvious choice' crap."

"He's my boss and my dad's oldest friend," she said in a harsh whisper.

"Some friend. He hasn't stepped up to spin the story away from suicide or squelch the other rumors. Wasn't it you who just yesterday called him a bastard?" So maybe he had overdone it a bit, but the guy had made him as mad as hell. Sam Maguire, as her father's oldest friend, should want to protect her. He should be on her side, listening and supporting her. Instead he was acting like an ass.

Jana opened her mouth, then clamped her lips together as new voices filled the outer office. Dylan recognized Rose's voice, but not the deeper voice of the man chatting with her.

On a quiet, frustrated groan, Jana moved away from Dylan as the visitor walked into her office without so much as a knock.

"Jana, you—" The gentle smile on the man's face

evaporated as he saw and sized up Dylan. "I do apologize. I wasn't aware you were in a meeting."

Dylan openly assessed him as well. The file on Jana hadn't mentioned any romantic ties, but this man gave off definite possessive signals. When Jana failed to make introductions, Dylan stuck out his hand. "Dylan Parker. Old college pal of Jana's."

"Gregory Atkins," he responded, shaking Dylan's hand. "I've never heard of you."

"Gregory is a friend of the family," Jana explained when the guy continued to stare at them. "What brings you by?"

Gregory moved in on her but Jana sidestepped, returning to her desk chair. Gregory didn't take the hint, coming around to her side and leaning in. "Have you heard about the appointment?"

"Sam just told me. Dylan and I were about to invite Camille out for a celebration dinner."

News to him. Dylan sat down with the philosophy book to watch the show.

"Do that after the swearing in," Gregory suggested. "We have plans tonight, remember? It's Friday."

Jana's smile wobbled. "It would be best if we rescheduled."

"I disagree. You need to get out and take a break from all of this. You cancelled the past two Fridays. It's time to start living again, sweetheart."

Sweetheart? Dylan bit back a growl of derision. Clearly Jana didn't consider herself this guy's sweetheart. Nothing in the file Claudia provided mentioned a boyfriend. Who the hell did he think he was?

"Gregory—"

"I made reservations at our favorite restaurant."

The man took self-absorbed to a new level. Curious, Dylan set the book aside and picked up his cell to skim Jana's file, double-checking for any mention of this guy. Nothing. Dylan searched the web for more details while Gregory wheedled and Jana evaded. An attorney, Atkins currently worked in the state prosecutor's office. It seemed he checked all the boxes of a proper background, but hadn't made a name for himself yet. Dylan pegged him as a man on the political ladder looking to land himself a senator's daughter and skip some of the grunt work.

"All right," Jana finally caved. "But I'll meet you at the restaurant." She cut off his protests, walking him out.

A moment later, she returned with their lunch, shutting her door and throwing the lock.

"You okay?" Dylan asked, taking the food cartons out of the sack. "Salad?"

She nodded. "Good thing, too. Apparently I'm having a big dinner." She sighed, flipping open the take-out container. "I assume you'll drop me off?"

He nodded. And he'd stay to keep an eye on things, but he wouldn't mention that now. "Why does Atkins think you belong to him?"

She scowled into her salad as she drizzled it with a mere trace of honey mustard dressing. "He wasn't in the file?"

Her surprise set off warning bells. "Should he be?" Dylan asked.

"I don't think so." She stabbed her fork into the greens. "You Googled him, didn't you?"

"Yes, though I didn't really need to. He smelled like an attorney." Dylan took a bit too much pleasure in her burst of laughter.

"Gregory's a decent guy. Dad and Camille think the world of him." Her face fell as she realized she should have used the past tense when it came to how her dad had felt.

"Another of those polite and useful political connections?" Dylan inquired, in hopes of drawing her thoughts away from the hurt.

"Yes."

"What do *you* think of him?"

Finally, she looked up from her salad, her soft green eyes a little sad. "He's nice. Well-groomed, socially speaking. Polite. Kind."

"Sounds like a winner," Dylan replied "And?"

"And... nothing. He's a friend who's worried about me, that's all."

"Did you tell him about the letter?"

She shook her head and poked at her salad, moving chunks of tomatoes in line with olives.

Great. Mr. Polite shows up and she'd reverted back to melancholy with no appetite. Although Dylan thought the man's whining could turn anyone's stomach.

"You're not going to tell me anything else are you?"

Another shake of her dark head. "He's an open book. Anything you want to know is easy to find online."

"Challenge accepted."

She didn't laugh this time. From investigative experience he assumed her reticence meant Gregory did actually fall into one of two categories: former lover or current lover. In her shoes, Dylan wouldn't be eager to admit to such bad judgment either. "Where's he taking you tonight?"

"Cavelli's. The toughest place in town to get a table. It's my job to be impressed, knowing he called in a favor for the reservation."

"Are you impressed?"

She gave him a false, toothy smile. "Naturally."

Remembering the key in his pocket, Dylan changed the subject. "Any idea what this is?" He placed the key on the table between them.

Frowning, she turned it over, and gave it back to him. "I've never seen it before. Where'd you find it?"

Dylan tipped his head toward the senator's office. "I guess this will keep me busy while you're living it up tonight." That brought a tiny, real smile to her lips.

He counted it a victory.

Seeing her smile had become important to him in record time.

CHAPTER 7

THROUGH THE REST of the afternoon, Jana did her best to ignore Dylan as he sorted through the fractured details they were trying to weave into a viable case for murder. She understood her dad's logic behind keeping the hate mail, but she couldn't come up with a valid explanation for hiding a key. Shaped like a safety deposit box key, the number didn't match the safety deposit box where her dad's will and other documents were stored.

Dylan hadn't wanted to discuss where in the office he'd found it any more than she'd wanted to discuss dinner with Gregory. They'd reached an impasse. Which left her with no distraction against Sam's announcement.

Jana hadn't really expected the appointment to her dad's seat, but she would've expected better reasons than the pressure would be too much for her. She couldn't think of a single moment since her father's death that would lead the governor to consider her fragile. Certainly he'd had no reason prior to her father's death. The reasoning simply didn't make sense. While Camille had hidden, Jana had handled everything without a public breakdown. She sighed, frustrated all over again.

"You okay?" Dylan asked.

She didn't bother to look up from the report she was drafting for Camille. "Fine." As the interim senator, her stepmother would need to catch up quickly. Where Jana should be seeing words, charts, and analyses, the blasted key kept popping into her head. Maybe her father had kept more than one safety deposit box. "I'd like to stop by the bank on the way home," she announced, this time risking eye contact with Dylan.

Her refusal to simply tell him about her history with Gregory made no sense whatsoever. Yet, somehow she couldn't bring herself to start that conversation.

Dylan met her gaze from across the room, his intense assessment making the space seem much smaller. "We can do that, but shouldn't Gregory pick up the dinner check?"

"Ha, ha." She dreaded having dinner with Gregory. Keeping him at arm's length tonight would be particularly challenging when she had more important things on her mind. Why wouldn't he take 'no' for an answer? And why would he choose now to blow a favor for a reservation at Cavelli's? He was usually so careful about his decisions and certainly never went out of his way for Jana. Playing second fiddle to his career had been a huge part of their relationship's demise—not that it was ever really much of a relationship anyway.

On a wave of anxiety, she pushed back from her desk and started shoving papers into her briefcase. "Is it a problem for you if we leave now?"

Dylan gave her another long look. "Not at all." He closed his laptop and set the books on top of her purse.

"Gee, thanks."

"Not enough room." He patted his computer bag, then held out his free hand for her purse. "I'll carry it."

"I've got it." She shook her head. "It doesn't match your boots."

As they walked out, Rose wished her well on her date and Jana cringed. "Does everyone know Gregory's taking me out?"

"It's Cavelli's." Rose winked at her. "All of Texas is waiting for Twitter updates," she said. "You're lovely together and you need to live a little. There's been talk since the two of you were introduced."

"It was cotillion!" Jana bit back the irritable rant hovering on the tip of her tongue as she left the office. She chose the back stairs, determined to avoid this strange new mix of sympathy for her loss and hope that she was moving on with her life that people were tossing at her lately.

Her father had been dead sixteen days and she was expected to move on and live a little? With *Gregory*? He wanted to marry her, but she didn't want *him*. "Absurd," she muttered, fuming until another thought struck her like a blow. She stopped short, trying to get her breath.

Her father wouldn't be at her wedding, no matter the name of her groom or when the ceremony occurred.

"Easy," Dylan said. "Not every Texan is talking about your date tonight."

"Th-that's not it." Her entire body quaked and a strange heat rushed up from her toes. "Oh, God." Her vision blurred and ringing filled her ears. Suddenly Dylan was easing her down to sit on the steps next to her purse and briefcase.

"Breathe," he said, crouching in front of her on the step below.

"I am." Maybe. She was trying anyway.

"Slower," he amended.

"You better move," she said, forcing each word past the lump in her throat.

"Are you feeling sick?"

"No. I might cry." To her astonishment, he chuckled, shifting to sit next to her. He rubbed her shoulders in gentle strokes. When she could get the words past her lips, she blurted. "Dad won't be at my wedding."

"You're engaged? To Gregory?"

She shook her head. "My wedding to anyone." Swiping tears from her cheeks, she felt the shock easing away with every touch of Dylan's hand. "With the whole," she flicked her hands, "mystery surrounding his death going on, I haven't thought about the future like holidays or... or other milestones."

"Those things sneak up on you," he said, drawing her close.

She couldn't remember anyone else taking this same care with her. Sure friends and colleagues expressed their sympathy, offered assistance, brought food, but they'd also looked to her to be strong, to make the decisions. That was what Jana Clayton always did. She'd done the majority of her grieving alone.

Leaning into his embrace, she inhaled the warm, woodsy scent that clung to his clothing. "Thank you."

"No big deal." He squeezed her shoulder and eased back just a bit, as if testing her balance. "Hard to believe, but I don't get my bonus if you faint and tumble down the stairs."

On a shaky laugh, she pulled herself up and decided the worst had passed.

"Better?" he asked, clearly ready to catch her if necessary.

She nodded. "Much better."

He gathered up everything, insisting she use the hand rail the rest of the way downstairs. "What's cotillion?" he asked when they were settled in his truck.

"A society thing designed to torture, I mean *teach* manners and social graces to teenagers," she explained. "It's weekly lessons learning how to navigate everything from a shrimp fork to the waltz."

"Sounds barbaric."

"There were days it sure felt that way," she agreed.

"Is that when Gregory proposed?"

She knew he was teasing her, but he should be aware. "The proposal came three months ago."

The truck came to an abrupt halt, just shy of the exit gate. "What?"

She stared at him, surprised by his dark expression. It clearly irritated him when she revealed things that weren't in the background file. "Your agency didn't miss anything. It's not public knowledge. Dad didn't even know. Gregory and I have been on again off again *friends* for years. Mostly because we were both busy and very focused on work. For the past year or so we've had a standing dinner engagement on Fridays. I guess I always thought it was to keep either of us from being alone on a Friday night. As for the unexpected proposal, I'll be forever grateful Gregory chose a private setting to ask."

"You said no." Dylan put the truck into motion once more.

She laced her fingers in her lap. "It's more accurate that I didn't say yes. The ring's in a drawer at home. I asked for some time and the next thing I knew my father was dead." She sighed. "He refuses to take the ring back."

"Whiny Greg has a spine?"

"It's more that he has a vision for his future," she said. Knowing she was wanted for her connections wasn't the same as being wanted. "He's generally irrelevant to the case. Where did you find that key?"

"Hidden in a star statue on the office bookshelf."

"Weird. Hopefully the bank will cooperate."

But shortly after they arrived, the bank manager explained their internal numbering system didn't match the key. Though she leaned hard on the longstanding family friendship, the manager couldn't—or wouldn't—offer any suggestions or insight.

With more sympathy for her loss echoing in Jana's ears, they left the bank and headed for her house. "What now?" she asked Dylan. "Am I supposed to just traipse into every local bank and ask?"

"That might raise more eyebrows and twitter trends than you and Gregory at Cavelli's."

"Stop it," she said without any real ire. "What do you suggest?"

"Let me do a little legwork. Claudia, my technical assistant, can run it down."

"Okay. I'll search Dad's papers for other banking connections."

He turned into her driveway. "Have you considered it might not be his key?"

She hadn't considered that at all. "Then why would it be in his office?"

"Beats me," Dylan said, following her into the house. "We'll figure it out."

Looking at her watch, she decided she had almost two hours before she had to dress for dinner. "Maybe we'll find something helpful before I have to leave."

Dylan poured her a glass of wine as they sat down at her kitchen table.

She sagged back in the chair, swirling the dark red liquid in the glass. "You don't have to drive. I can always take a cab."

"I do have to drive." His tone left no room for argument. "Have you forgotten those two attempts on your life? I won't interfere with your friendly date."

"It's not that."

"Then what? I promise I'll be as close as a text message."

"Nothing." She felt her cheeks heating and she reached for the book full of hate mail. "It's just strange." It barely qualified as an explanation, but she couldn't find the right words to describe the turmoil inside her. Knowing he'd be watching her gave her goose bumps. It should've been creepy, instead she relished the unexpected thrill.

"You can do better than that."

She stared at him across the kitchen table. "Maybe I don't want to."

Those blue eyes held hers and she refused to look away. "Suit yourself," he said. Using his cell phone to take a picture of both sides of the key, he seemed to shift seamlessly into investigative mode.

She did her best to follow his example, until the alarm she'd set went off. Reluctantly, she left the hate mail she'd been trying to coordinate with legislative voting records and went to dress for dinner.

Rummaging under her lingerie for the slim box where she kept her mother's pearls, her fingers bumped a smaller velvet box. She pulled it out and opened it. The sparkling diamond felt so heavy, so permanent, and it wasn't even on her finger.

Her girlfriends would've bubbled over with envy and happiness at the sight of this gorgeous ring, but she had yet to experience anything other than dread when she looked at it.

Gregory was nice enough. Accomplished. Connected. But he wasn't…

Dylan.

She snapped the box closed and dropped it back into the drawer as if it held the next plague. How could a couple of days, hard words, a harder body, and only the smallest kindnesses mean more to her than a man she'd known most of her life? *What would Dad think of Dylan?* The question startled her almost as much as the immediate answer: the two of them would've gotten along well.

Her phone sounded another alarm and with a final glance at her reflection, she dropped the device into her evening clutch and walked back to the kitchen.

"You're sure you don't mind giving me a ride?"

"If you drove yourself, I'd have to follow you and..." Dylan's voice trailed off as he looked up from his laptop.

He stared at her for so long, she started to worry she'd overdone it. "What's wrong?"

DYLAN GOT TO HIS FEET, belatedly remembering his manners. He closed his computer with a snap and shoved it back into the bag along with the hate mail from the book.

"You look stunning."

She scowled at him and her chin came up as if she was ready to deflect an insult.

What the hell was a man supposed to say when a woman walked in looking like that? The black dress hugged her curves, stopping just above her knees. Her hair was up, but she'd done it differently, and the effect was softer with a few loose curls framing her face. The black heels were sexy as hell, but the pearls gave off a classy, good-girl vibe.

"I'm ready," he said. *For anything*, he thought with a great deal of regret, helping her into her coat. Whatever fragrance she'd applied was feminine but understated and nothing like her stepmother's power scent. He decided the original Mrs. Clayton had influenced Jana more than Camille. Did she realize that?

As they drove away from her neighborhood, he couldn't believe he was delivering Jana to a date with another man. She wasn't his, wouldn't want to be his, but his unexpected spike of jealousy was real enough.

"What will you do about dinner?" she asked, fidgeting with her small, sparkling purse.

"I'll work. I grabbed a frozen dinner while you were dressing." He kept his eyes on the road when they wanted to wander over her again. "Claudia's blocked out time for me, us, *your case* tonight." Good grief. Horny teenagers on first dates didn't get more flustered than he felt right now. He didn't know what it was about her, but if he got distracted, she could get hurt. He checked the mirrors for motorcycles or other aggressive activity and pulled himself together. "If there's any connection between the hate mail and the people who were closest to your dad, we'll find it."

"*Hmm.*"

"Have you thought of something new?"

"No." He caught her drumming her fingers on her bare knee. "It's just a challenge labeling suspects knowing you're right about who had access to the study."

A terrible thought occurred to him. One he should've had hours ago. "Does Gregory have a motive?"

Her fingers went still and she turned toward him,

but she didn't immediately defend the man. Dylan counted it progress. He knew what she was going through, having been blinded and betrayed so completely by a woman he'd loved.

"I can't think of a valid motive for Gregory to want to harm Dad. He did have insider access," she admitted, "but Dad's support increased his very slim chances of marrying me which makes me think he would have wanted Dad around."

Dylan pulled the truck into the line for the valet at the restaurant. "I thought you refused him."

She reached up, checking her earring. "Honestly, the idea of becoming Mrs. Gregory Atkins makes me cringe. I wanted to marry for love like my parents, but I've learned not everyone is lucky enough to find someone both appropriate *and* lovable."

Appropriate. The valet opened her door on that shocking statement. "I'll let Gregory bring me home."

Whiny Greg stood just inside the restaurant waiting for her. Dylan suddenly didn't want to let her go. "Just a minute—"

She patted his arm. "Relax. It's the right compromise."

"I'm as close as a text message," he reminded her as she closed the door. "Damn it." He pulled away from the restaurant and circled the block, searching for the best place to park and keep an eye on her.

"Going soft, Parker," he scolded himself. A pretty, smart woman dressed to kill talking about murder suspects and marrying for love in practically the same breath was a heady combination.

The spurt of jealousy amid the general apathy about his personal life took him by surprise. It was his fault he'd passed thirty a couple years back without any prospect of a wife or family. Considering his current employment status, he couldn't see his prospects improving.

Why should anything change? He didn't need the wife and kids and a dog lounging on perfect, green grass behind a white-picket fence. He liked his job. He even liked the attorney who'd hauled him out of that San Antonio jail cell and pushed a Guardian Agency contract under his nose. More importantly, he was good at this job. He kept people alive and leveled the playing field when circumstances were off balance. Right now, it was his job to make sure Jana survived long enough to turn her professional and personal goals into a reality.

He should be in that restaurant, eyes on her. It was protocol. For a moment, he debated blowing off Claudia and doing just that. He knew how to convince people to let him have a small dark corner to complete an assignment.

Who knew what Gregory was capable of or who he was cooperating with?

Dylan gave himself a mental kick. Gregory might be a pawn, but unless Claudia had news to the contrary, he wasn't any real threat. Based on Jana's self-defense efforts last night, Dylan thought she could take down Gregory if necessary. He had the make and model of Gregory's car, had eyes on the only exit from the parking lot. If Gregory or anyone else went after her, Dylan could intervene.

His phone hummed with a text message from Jana. The smiley face left him wondering how she knew he needed confirmation of her safety. Another text came through, this one from an unfamiliar number: It's Swede. In town if you need me.

Well, that was something positive. He'd reply as soon as he was done with his meeting with Claudia. Pushing a hand through his short hair, he pulled out his computer. He only had to wait a few minutes. "Tell me you have something," he said just as soon as she came online.

"Hello, Parker. I take it your surly mood means the client didn't find anything helpful in the hate mail?"

"No," Dylan replied. "And my mood is fine."

"If you say so," she replied. "What you've sent me is too general. And old."

"Great," Dylan mumbled. "Anything on the key?"

"Yes, actually."

Dylan heard the click and skitter of her fingers racing over her keyboard, but she didn't say anything. "And?"

"I'm getting there. Whatever it is, it's not related to any of the banks in the Austin area. Wait." That familiar tapping of the keys echoed. "It matches one used by a small Texas bank that closed thirty years ago."

Damn it. "You're sure?"

"Seriously?" she asked, her voice flat.

"Sorry." Questioning Claudia's research was high-risk proposition. He caught a flash of movement in his side mirror. "I appreciate your hard work," he added quickly, watching for any other movement. "I may have to cut this short."

"What's wrong?"

Two men dressed in dark clothing were converging on the truck. A smart man would hope they were simply headed out to the social action on Sixth Street, but Dylan wouldn't mind a place to unload some of the pent up frustration this case was causing. "Just business, Claudia. I'll check in later." Dylan closed the laptop and slid it across the seat, under his hat. The men were too close to take time to text Swede. He rested his hand on the butt of his the weapon holstered at his side beneath his jacket.

At his tailgate, the two men separated, coming up on either side of the cab. The man at the driver's side window rapped on the glass and motioned for him to step out of the truck. Dylan barely kept the eager smile in check.

"What's the problem?" he asked through the glass.

"Just want a word," the man—the Talker, Dylan decided—said.

"Sure thing." Dylan looked to the guy hovering at the passenger window and then back to the man on his side of the truck. He powered down the glass about half way. "What word do you want?"

"Can you step out of the truck?" Talker stepped back, giving him room.

"Do I need to?"

"Yes."

The quiet guy, Silent Partner, at the passenger window tested the door handle. Dylan shot him a look.

"We haven't seen you in Austin before," Talker said.

"It's a big place," Dylan replied.

"We think you should leave town."

"Really?"

Silent Partner tested the door handle again.

Dylan tipped his head that way. "Are you talking for him, too?"

"You aren't welcome here. Jana Clayton doesn't need you hanging around, pestering her. Leave right now and no one gets hurt."

Dylan wanted to laugh. "I'm a librarian," he lied. "I'm gathering information for Senator Clayton's memorial at the university library."

This declaration apparently stumped both men for a second, then Talker shot a hand through the open window, grabbing Dylan's collar in a ham-sized fist.

Dylan was ready. Manacling the bastard's hand, he opened the door and slammed it hard into his chest.

Immediately, Silent Partner tried for the door handle again, but Dylan hadn't hit the unlock button. Unless they smashed the windows, everything inside the truck was safe. Using his bodyweight, Dylan brought the guy's wrist down hard on the doorframe. Talker screamed and Dylan dropped down, sweeping the man's legs out from under him.

Talker rolled away, cradling his wrist, just in time for Silent Partner to charge into the fray.

"Round two." Dylan dodged a big roundhouse punch and drove his elbow into the man's windpipe.

If the guy had ever possessed the power of speech, it was muted now. He tried again to plow Dylan into his truck, but his fist met metal rather than flesh. "Ouch," Dylan taunted. "Bet that hurts," he added, driving a knee into his kidney.

Talker was back up on his feet and swearing. Dylan caught a glancing blow on the side of his face and swore right back as blood dripped onto his best white shirt.

"Who sent you?" he demanded trading punches with Talker and guarding any access to the truck. Neither man replied, so Dylan started tossing out names. "Maguire? Camille? Atkins?" It was hard to read reactions in the dark amid wild swings and strikes. "Any chance you two are into motorcycles?"

He didn't think the answer would've been yes even if this pair was inclined to talk. The motorcycle crew would've come in armed and shot him at the first sign of resistance. He wasn't sure what that meant about the person who hired this pair of incompetent bullies.

Growing bored, Dylan upped his game and with a few smart, swift moves and both men went down and stayed down. "Thanks for the workout," he said, climbing back into his truck. "Tell your boss I'm staying right here in Austin as long as it suits me."

He started the truck and pulled out of the parking space, not too worried about whether or not he ran over his assailants. They didn't seem the type to press charges. Dylan pulled up to the Cavelli's valet stand and gave the kid twenty bucks to keep his truck close. Then he walked around to the kitchen entrance of the restaurant. Everyone was too busy to notice him so he planted himself at the door where he had a good look at the dining room.

Spotting Jana and Gregory at a cozy table near the front window, he pulled out his phone and sent her a smile with a question mark. He watched her react, more than a little pleased when he got a smile followed by a bored face.

He'd update Claudia later. And reach out to Swede. After that pathetic attempt at intimidation, he wouldn't let Jana out of his sight again.

Even bozos could be dangerous sometimes.

CHAPTER 8

J ANA WALKED into her house and locked the door, watching from the window until Gregory finally drove away. A moment later, she saw Dylan's truck roll by and turn at the corner. It had been such a relief to know he was close, not because she feared Gregory, but after being attacked twice she was a little paranoid. Throughout the evening she'd hyper analyzed every word out of Gregory and checked her surroundings for anyone too interested in her, despite Dylan's assurances that he was close.

Exhausted now, she slipped out of her heels and headed back to her bedroom. Dinner had been such a drain, as the primary topic was the governor's appointment. Gregory meant well, but she resented giving him time when she could've been working on finding the person who'd shot her father. And she kept hearing Dylan's voice in her head calling him Whiny Greg. How had she overlooked that tendency all these years?

She turned on the bedside lamp and reached back to

unzip her dress. If Gregory refused to let her return the engagement ring in person, she'd have it delivered. She couldn't allow him to keep hoping she'd eventually say yes.

Replacing her shoes in the organizer, she dropped her dress into the dry cleaning bag, and slipped her favorite silky nightshirt over her head. When she finished washing her face and brushing her hair, she saw her phone flashing with an alert.

She read the text message from Dylan confirming he was in place for the night and asking if she was okay. After sending him another smiley face, she slid between the covers. She reached up to turn out the light and spotted something that chilled her to the bone. She grabbed her phone and took a picture of the thin black wire peeking from the edge of the lampshade.

What now? If it was an electronic bug she would tip off the listener if she reacted. She sat up a little and tried to think past the overwhelming sense of being violated. Someone had been in her home. She needed to tell Dylan, but how could she let him know without alerting whoever was listening?

She could wait until morning and talk it over with him in the safety of his truck. Her eyes drifted back to the wire and she knew she couldn't tolerate the privacy invasion for even one night. She eased out of bed, taking her phone along as she crept back to the front room. If there was one bug, there were likely more.

What if her cell phone was tapped too? How could she get Dylan in here? She forced herself away from the edge of panic. A walk in the backyard had brought him running last night, she might as well try it again. Opening the sliding door off the kitchen, she stepped out into the night. The cold air blasted across her legs and under her nightshirt, but she refused to waste time going back for a coat or shoes. Dylan would be here soon enough. She paced to the far edge of the patio, imagining hot coals as her feet protested against the cold concrete.

Minutes ticked by and Dylan didn't show up. Worried something had happened to him, she started around the side of the house in search of his truck. A hand shot out of the dark, catching her upper arm in a warm, firm grasp. She recognized the touch, his scent. "Dylan," she said, relief washing over her.

"Where are you going?"

"I need you," she whispered.

"What?" His hand dropped away and the air temperature seemed to drop even more.

She showed him the picture on her phone. "Someone bugged my house." She tried to decipher his expression in the faint light of her phone, but it was impossible to guess his thoughts.

He ushered her quickly back to the patio door. "Wait right there," he murmured, nudging her across the threshold. "I'm bringing the truck around."

"Okay." She left the sliding door cracked a bit as he jogged off. Moments later, she heard the rumble of an engine approaching and headlights sliced across the side of the house as he pulled into her driveway.

Her phone hummed with a text message: Open the front door

She closed the slider as quietly as possible and hurried through the house to let him in. Under the porch light she imagined greeting a man in her emerald nightshirt made quite an impression if anyone was watching. Worse now that she saw he was carrying an overnight bag along with his computer bag. These rumors would be fun to live down during a political campaign. God, she was so sick of all the pretenses and precautions.

"Are you okay?" He locked the door, then dropped the bags and flipped on the foyer light.

She gasped when she saw his face. He had a bruise welling on his cheekbone, a split lip and blood on his shirt. "What happened to you?"

He waved off her question, kneeling to retrieve something from the bigger bag. "Some guy tried to hustle me." He gave her a big wink and tapped his ear. "It didn't go his way."

She knew it was a lie since he'd been watching her all night. Following his lead, she kept up her end of the conversation about his fictitious evening as he walked through every room in the house, pointing out several bugs.

Shivering, she rubbed her hands up and down her arms, giving serious thought to donning fuzzy socks for her freezing toes. It wouldn't help. She could crank up the heat, but the chill she felt didn't come from temperature.

"I could use a shower first," Dylan said suddenly. "If you don't mind."

Her mind tripped over 'shower' and stalled out at

the implication of 'first' before she realized he was still making the conversation sound good for the listeners. The guest bathroom wasn't bugged, but Dylan started the shower anyway.

"What do we do?" she said when he closed the door.

Dylan leaned back against the vanity countertop. "You've never noticed anything like this before?"

She shook her head.

"The whole house is bugged. You couldn't have missed all of them for any length of time. Someone must have done this while you were out tonight. Did Atkins seem to be stalling at dinner? Did he use his phone at all?"

"Cavelli's isn't known for speedy service." She thought back through the evening. "If he checked his phone, he was subtle about it."

"There might've been another signal," Dylan said. "How do you want to play this?"

She had no idea. Of course she understood criminal cases where people were under legally-authorized surveillance, but that didn't apply here. "What are my options?"

"Leave them in place and be very careful to reveal details on purpose."

"You're suggesting we use the devices against whoever planted them."

Dylan nodded.

"Or?" The bathroom was starting to steam up. While the heat felt good, she was self-conscious about her nightshirt clinging to her body.

"Or I can disable them right now."

"Do that."

"All right," he said slowly. "But that reduces our chances of learning who planted them."

"I understand." She rubbed a hand up and down her arm, smoothing away the goose bumps that kept racing across her skin, thanks to Dylan's proximity. "I can't stand the idea of someone listening to my every move."

With a nod, he walked out of the bathroom. She turned off the water and followed him.

"Why don't you pour us a drink," he said loudly enough for every bug in the house to pick it up. "We'll celebrate."

She shot him a dark look before heading for the kitchen. Who did he think he was baiting? She got him a beer, not because he'd asked, but because she thought his face could use it.

"You're lucky they missed your nose," she said, studying the bruising as he systematically destroyed the listening devices scattered around her house.

"Lucky, that's me." His grin was wicked, straining the cut on his lip. He tipped back the beer bottle for a long drink and handed it back to her. "Hold that one more second."

He aimed a small electronic device at another bug and with an ornery sneer, he turned the knob.

She winced at the high-pitched squeal, but it was over quickly. "You didn't do that with the others," she said, rubbing at her ear.

"I did," he said, "just not as loudly. Zapping the last one is always fun." He took the beer out of her hand, tipping it back for another long swallow.

She shouldn't be staring at the strong column of his neck. Shouldn't be fascinated by the spatter of blood on his shirt or his scraped up knuckles.

"You can speak freely now."

"Someone jumped you because of me," she said.

"I asked, but they didn't confirm." He shrugged. "It's a perk of the job."

"Perk?" Good grief what an absolutely *male* attitude. "Come with me." She caught his arm and headed back to the guest bathroom.

"The house is clean," he said, when she turned on the sink.

"*You* are not. Sit down," she added when he narrowed his gaze. Those blue eyes turned hot with speculation. "I mean it. This isn't a fight you'll win."

DYLAN OBEYED, sitting on the edge of the bathtub. His hands full of the beer and bug killer, he wondered what she planned to do. He watched her pull washcloths and a first aid kit from under the sink and groaned. "It's nothing. No need to go to all this trouble."

He didn't need an impromptu nurse tending to him and he sure as hell didn't need the torture of close quarters when she was dressed—or rather undressed—like that. The deep emerald fabric slithered over her body in a ripple of light and shadow playing with the soft curves of her breasts and hips. Much shorter than the black dress had been, he was getting an eye-full of her toned legs. Her long, chestnut hair was caught up in a clip at the back of her head. It was all too easy to imagine tugging out that fragile hold and letting that glossy mane tumble over her shoulders. He could practically feel how it would brush his face if she bent close to kiss him. He shifted, trying to hide the erection coming on fast.

"Hold still," she muttered, picking up his hand to deal with his scraped knuckles. She took the nearly empty beer bottle from him and set it aside, then did the same with the bug zapper.

"I can take care of myself," he grumbled.

"I'm sure you have all kinds of experience." She didn't seem inclined to let him prove it. She washed one hand, then the other, smoothing some flowery salve across his battered flesh.

"What is that?"

"Lavender oil and aloe."

"Huh?"

"It won't unman you." Her eyes were locked onto his mouth. In another context, with another woman, he'd think she wanted to kiss him.

She reached toward his fat lip with that damned cloth and he caught her wrist. "I'll do it." There was only so much a man could take.

She propped her hand on her hip, watching him wipe away the dried blood. "Take off your shirt."

"Excuse me?"

"You take care of your face and I'll deal with the bloodstain."

"Just trash it. I have other shirts."

"With you?"

She'd caught him there. He needed to get a handle on the situation before his hands landed on her. "Whoever bugged your house is likely to escalate quickly now that we've killed them."

"Escalate?" Her dark eyebrows rose. "Dad's dead, they've taken a couple shots at me, and beat you up."

"The hell they did." He lurched to his feet and turned to the mirror. She hovered behind him, her hands planted on those sweet hips. It brought the fabric tight across her breasts. "I guarantee you the two of them look a hell of a lot worse than me."

"Hooray." She let out a patently false cheer. "Give me the shirt."

"Fine." If she wanted the damn shirt, she could have it. He dropped the washcloth onto the counter with a splat and turned around. Her green eyes watched his fingers work through each button, going wide when faced with his bare chest. He thrust the fabric at her. "Here."

She took the shirt, but didn't leave as he'd hoped. The bathroom, technically spacious, felt way too small when she looked up at him like that. Her gaze drifted down, over his torso as soft and curious as a caress. Her fingers fluttered close to his ribs before she snatched back her hand. "You'll have bruises."

"Typical result when body blows are exchanged." She couldn't really care this much about what happened to him.

"I have something for it," she said.

"Me too," he said. "My kit is in the truck."

"Dylan."

He waited, trying to ignore the ache in his chest and the ache building quite a bit lower, as she stared at him.

"I—" She dropped his shirt and reached for his face, bringing his mouth to hers. The kiss was gentle, cautious, and nowhere near enough of what he wanted.

She tasted sweet, but nothing close to innocent. Sweet and cool like a peppermint candy. Her lips, her touch, her scent all of it washed over him. Forgetting his fat lip, he slanted his mouth across hers and speared his fingers deep into all that hair. The clip fell, jangling across the tile floor, and her silky tresses tumbled free. It felt even better than he imagined.

Licking the seam of her lips, he went for it, stroking her tongue with his the moment she opened for him. Their breath mingled and his heart pounded as her soft curves molded to his body. His palms learned her shape, dipping in at her waist, following the luscious flare of her hips. He smoothed his hands across the satin fabric to the hem and then under the nightshirt. Her skin was warm and soft and for several long, delicious minutes he couldn't think of anything but how her legs would feel wrapped around his hips while he buried himself deep inside her.

The image in his brain shocked him out of the passionate stupor. He broke the kiss and, with his hands on her waist, set her away, giving them both a little distance. He wouldn't apologize, but he couldn't continue. Not when he wanted to get her naked and keep her that way for a few hours. Or days. Weeks might be enough.

What a hot mess.

He pushed a hand through his hair and struggled for the right words. "I need to update Claudia." She'd be furious that he'd basically hung up on her twice tonight. Once before the fight and once when he'd spotted Jana in the yard. In nothing but a nightgown. *Christ.*

"Claudia." she echoed.

"My assistant." He squeezed out of the tight space between Jana's body and the counter top. "She's my technical contact. I'll just go—"

"Hold on."

He froze, waiting.

"We were, *um*, making out and you were thinking of *her?*"

"Yes." Her face fell. "No." He shook his head. The words weren't coming out right.

"Yes or no?" she queried.

Was that a smile tugging the corner of her mouth? "No." He roped his thoughts back in line before they ran away with his ability to think logically again. "I'll be right back."

"You can't go outside without your shirt," she called after him.

"No one's awake enough to care," he said.

"I am."

He groaned, thought about banging his head against the wall. Turning, he faced her once more. "What do you want from me?"

"You can't sleep in your truck again. You need better rest after a fight."

"I sleep just fine out there."

"Take the guest room." She backed up a few paces

and reached into a doorway. The light came on in the designated room.

Only a few more steps would bring him to her bedroom. "That's not a good idea." He'd never be able to resist the temptation. Based on the kiss she'd laid on him, he wasn't sure she'd be smart enough to tell him no.

"Am I or am I not the client?"

He rolled his eyes. "I'm not your employee," he said, dodging the question.

"Answer me."

"Fine. You are the client."

"Is it your policy, as a company, to ignore client requests?"

He could see where she was headed with this. "In my industry the client is *not* always right because the client does not always have the experience or insight required to make an effective decision."

"You're sleeping in the guest room," she stated.

"No."

"Dylan this is silly."

"I agree. I'll be back in the morning."

"Fine, then we'll sleep in the truck together."

"No way." He spun around to argue, but she'd hurried up behind him and he nearly knocked her over. "That's not happening."

"I'm scared and I don't want to be alone."

"Bullshit."

Her chin came up and she crossed her arms. The hem of that sexy nightshirt crept higher, revealing another inch of her stunning thighs. This was torture. He forced his gaze to the ceiling.

"Please take the guest room," she said. "You need real rest."

As if he'd get any rest knowing she was right down the hall. After that kiss, he wasn't likely to get much rest parked in her driveway or anywhere. "Don't do this, Jana." She was transferring the stress into sexual attraction. Classic coping mechanism, but he could not cross that line with a client.

"Too late. Manners are part of the Clayton genetic code."

Manners. Right. "You won't drop this?"

She shook her head. "You decide. Your place or mine?"

He could take her to his hotel, but that would only put him in the same room with her and two beds. "Fine." He wouldn't survive the night if she came out to his truck wearing only that nightshirt. He stalked through the house, checking the door and window locks. Then he grabbed his gear from the foyer. Half-afraid to meet her gaze, he ignored her, going straight into the guest room.

She might claim to feel safer with him around, but he didn't share the sentiment. He felt safer going up against a couple of thugs than he did in this tastefully decorated guest room with Jana down the hall. He dropped his gear and had just unfastened his jeans when she knocked on the door.

He opened it about an inch. "What?"

"Thank you."

He was no match for the sheer relief shining in her eyes. "You're welcome."

"And about that kiss…"

He closed his eyes and dropped his head against the door frame. "Yeah?" Would she dump the blame on him, claim temporary insanity, or make him an offer he'd have to refuse?

"Are you involved with anyone? Romantically," she added. "Like Claudia."

"No." He nearly laughed. Lately, the rare times he 'involved' himself with a woman, it was all about mutual satisfaction. "Are you?"

Her green gaze locked with his, warm and open. "I believe I am now."

He watched her turn away, her footsteps soft as she disappeared into her room while he stood there trying to figure out what the hell she meant. Maybe cleaning his bloody knuckles and kissing his split lip had proved to her she was better off with Gregory. The idea left him snarling with jealousy, but he'd get over it.

He had to. Women as classy as Jana Clayton didn't think long-term when they looked at rough-edged men like him. Hell, after the fiasco in Montana he didn't want to think long-term about any kind of woman.

But that wouldn't keep him from dreaming about her.

CHAPTER 9

SATURDAY, *November 17*

Reaching the state house early the next morning under a crystalline-blue sky that looked far too happy for Jana's grim mood, they found more listening devices when they searched the office suite. "Who would do this?" she asked, frustrated as she watched Dylan destroy the bug on Rose's desk phone.

"They weren't here before," Dylan said.

It was hardly a helpful answer. "So why now?"

"Got a key for Maguire's office?" He wiggled the locked door handle.

She shook her head. "It doesn't matter," she replied. "If it's bugged I'll think he's innocent and you'll tell me he planted them to divert suspicion."

His eyes went wide. "You're a quick study."

"Yes, I am. I need to get Dad's papers in order for Camille in case things, ah, escalate."

He sat down in one of the reception chairs. "I'll run interference for you."

She rolled her eyes. "Thanks, but it's not necessary. It's Saturday. Things should be quiet around here today." She ducked into her dad's office and turned on the television to the local morning show. It felt cowardly, but she didn't have a choice. She was running out of time and access. There had to be a clue to the key and, potentially, the killer in the paperwork or on his computer. She refused to envision anything other than success. Her father hadn't killed himself and she'd prove it with Dylan's help.

A more confident woman would've said something about that kiss last night. She just didn't have the right words after another restless night of Dylan starring in her increasingly creative and erotic dreams. Lust and hormones could wait. The governor would announce Camille's appointment any time now and Jana would be there, showing her support.

She understood why Dylan suspected everyone. Just as she understood her resistance to the idea that she'd completely misjudged someone close to her father. Her cell phone hummed with an incoming text message as she skimmed through computer files, forwarding to her email address what she thought might be important to Dylan's investigation or Camille's assumption of her father's role as a legislator.

Recognizing Gregory's number she groaned, but she had no answer for the *Where are you?* message. As she debated her response, the television flashed a breaking news banner.

Her stomach dropped. "Dylan," she rasped. She tried

again, this time bringing him rushing into the office. Pointing to the television, she turned up the volume. Together they watched as Camille stood in the senate chamber taking her oath to fulfill Senator J.D. Clayton's seat for the remainder of his term.

"I should be there," she said, shutting down her search. "Rose is there." Gregory was there alongside the District Attorney. Sam stood at the edge of those gathered, a serious but pleased expression on his face.

"You'll never get there in time."

"It's not far. Why didn't they tell me?"

Dylan shook his head. "It's too late."

He was right, showing up late would be worse than not being there at all. Maybe it was for the best though she worried her absence would hurt Camille's reception as interim Senator. Everyone in the legislature knew how closely Jana had worked with her father on policy and issues while Camille had been involved with the charities, campaigns, and state events.

As Camille and Sam answered questions, Jana picked up her phone and sent a text message to Tammy Fowler, her counterpart in Senator Wagg's office. Senator Wagg had been serving almost as long as her dad and the men had been close friends and allies on many issues.

Dylan shuffled his feet, leaning back against the desk as the questions continued. "If it was so important to show a united front, why didn't Maguire tell you when to show up?"

"No idea." Her phone hummed and she saw a

response from Tammy. "Hopefully my friend will have some idea."

"Be careful," Dylan warned. "Can I help you finish up in here?"

She shook her head, exchanging text messages with Tammy who was eager to chat privately this afternoon. "We have a little time. She'll take questions for a few more minutes." And then what? Jana didn't have any idea.

To her relief, Dylan's phone rang, cutting through her jumbled thoughts. He stepped into Rose's office to answer it and she returned to the task at hand.

"Come on, Dad," she muttered aloud now that no one was listening. She scrolled through the inbox folder icon on his monitor once more. "Something was wrong and it apparently wasn't your marriage."

Jana had combed through his calendar, but couldn't find any red flags. Yet she knew her dad. He'd been unusually reticent in those last weeks. She forced herself to stop and think. When had that started? Pinpointing the first behavior shift could narrow the search field.

Voices carried into the office suite and no one sounded pleased to see Dylan. She was rising to go greet Camille when her stepmother walked in and closed the door firmly.

"You're in my chair," she said quietly. The twist of her lips couldn't be called a smile.

"Congratulations," Jana said, coming around to offer a hug. "I wish I'd known about the swearing in."

Camille stepped away quickly. "We're alone, Jana. You don't have to pretend."

"Pardon me?"

"I personally sent you the email invitation last night." She flicked her fingers. "This is a terribly difficult time for all of us. Sam smoothed over the gaffe for you."

"Thanks." Jana kept her voice even, but her temper rose. "I was just gathering some paperwork to make your transition easier."

"Thoughtful, but not necessary." Camille sank into the desk chair, smoothing her palms over the supple leather arm rests. "I'll have to make some changes," she said to herself. "The décor is far too masculine for me."

"Rose and I can help you with that."

"That's not necessary." Camille's smile was brittle. "I'll need you to turn over everything you've been working on. Projects, reports, assessments. Sam and I will prioritize the agenda for the next session."

"You'll have it in the morning, just as soon as I'm done putting it in order."

"You're done *now*, darling." Her smile turned sweet enough to cause cavities. "Don't you understand? I must bring in my own staff as soon as possible. With the holidays coming up, it's the perfect time for you to regroup and recover from losing your dad."

"You're firing me?"

"No!" Camille leaned forward, examining the papers Jana had gathered. "I'm giving you the freedom to take care of yourself. It's what a mother does."

"I see."

"Good. Everything on my desk by the end of the day.

I'd rather not cause a scene having security escort you out."

"That won't be necessary," Jana said through gritted teeth.

"I'm glad we understand each other." Camille shooed Jana away like a pesky fly. "Send Sam in on your way out."

"Yes, ma'am."

"That's 'Senator', please."

Appalled, unable to reconcile this woman with the Camille she'd known and respected, Jana opened the door and stepped out to a room full of cameras and media. She smiled automatically, expressing her delight at the appointment, though she couldn't be sure that was the question posed. Catching Sam's eye across the reception area, she signaled that his presence was requested by the new Senator Clayton. Then she squeezed through the crowd and quietly closed her office door, blocking out the media.

"What happened?" Dylan asked, looking up from the work table by the window.

"Nothing good." Jana looked at her desk, then the rest of the room. She was going to miss this place. "I decided to go into politics in eighth grade," she said. "Growing up in Dad's shadow, watching how much he cared about the people and the process inspired me. It colored every choice I've made my entire life. I fretted over every grade I made right up through my master's thesis."

"And here you are," Dylan said, closing his laptop. "You made it."

"For a few years," she agreed. The job had brought more challenges and joy than she'd anticipated. She was going to miss it. "There were whispers when Dad hired me as an advisor, but no one could argue with the work ethic that qualified me."

"What's wrong?"

She swallowed back tears, telling herself Camille's decision wasn't personal. "A career in politics is like planting in rocky soil. Dad said that ages ago," she explained. "Voters are fickle and careers are made and unmade on the smallest of decisions."

"Hang on." Dylan lowered his voice. "Camille fired you?"

"Sam implied the interim Senator might not keep me on."

"He said he didn't know who'd be appointed." Dylan joined her at the desk. "Answer me, Jana. Did she fire you?"

Jana shrugged. "Not exactly. The new senator has granted me a leave of absence to grieve properly." Where was the anger when she needed it? All she felt was empty.

"Bullshit." Dylan rocked back on his heels. "She didn't admit to murder or bugging your house and the office, did she?"

"We should be so lucky."

"Congratulations."

"For what?" She opened a drawer and pulled out the few personal items. Suddenly she would have given anything if she'd already cleared out her office.

"You finally suspect someone of acting against your dad. That's a big step."

"God help me if there are eleven more."

His half grin drew her attention to his mouth, made her want another kiss. She couldn't think of a better distraction for a newly unemployed social policy advisor.

"Why don't we just get out of here?" he offered, as if reading her mind.

"Camille—the senator—has demanded all the paperwork by the end of the day."

"Are you going to comply?"

"If I do she won't have security escort me out."

"How thoughtful of her," Dylan said with a heavy dose of sarcasm.

Jana snorted. "I have a meeting in a few hours. Let's use the time we have here to erase any search that isn't explained by the library thing."

"I guess this is our last chance to look for any clues that might help with our investigation."

"There has to be something here." Jana considered the possibilities—all of which they'd gone over at least once already. "If Dad had concerns he would've found a way to let me know."

"You're sure?"

"You don't stay in politics as long as Dad did without learning how to take precautions."

DYLAN HAD KNOWN the situation would likely escalate, but even he hadn't expected this sort of blowback. He was going to reach out to Swede at the next opportunity. They needed to make headway on this case sooner rather than later. He'd intended to tell her last night what he'd learned about the key, but the confrontation with the bozos had changed his agenda. Then that damned kiss had basically blown his mind.

He reached into his pocket and pulled out his flash drive. "Who handles data security and storage?"

"Why?"

"It might become relevant. I took this off of Rose's computer on our first visit. I'm betting if we looked at her computer now, there wouldn't be much there."

She pulled a similar flash drive from a miniscule pocket at the waistband of her straight skirt. "I had a similar thought." She handed it to him. "I also went through his email forwarding and deleting things that troubled me."

"More hate mail?"

"Not exactly." She turned on the television and started shredding a page or two out of each report she'd compiled for the new senator.

"You're not going to tell me."

"I will, but we have to make some progress here before my meeting."

"Fair enough. What's my job?"

"Gather up anything personal. All of the books. I'm calling a friend from security for boxes."

"Really?"

She gave him a hard look. "He'll be able to verify, if asked, that I didn't take anything valuable."

"What about the computer?" He asked when she'd completed the call. He packed his own computer and the hate mail, but he kept the flash drives in his shirt pocket. "Will she lock you out?"

"I'm sure Sam's already changed the passwords."

"You don't sound worried about it."

"One of the risks of hiring close family is that they know how you think."

Dylan stopped, an all-too-familiar sense of dread falling across his shoulders. Camille could flip this entire investigation on its ear, especially if she was behind the murder. He had a nagging feeling she'd orchestrated the senator's demise even if she didn't pull the trigger herself. "That means Camille will know how you think, too."

"Let's hope she keeps on believing that."

Dylan caught the absolute determination and temper sizzling in Jana's eyes. First impressions were rarely misleading, but with her, he had to recalculate too damn frequently. Was it the nature of politics or the nature of the woman? The trouble with Jana was that every new obstacle revealed a layer stronger than the last. He found her challenging and intoxicating.

You're walking a dangerous line, Parker.

She might consider her career path full of obstacles, but he was starting to see how those trials had forged her into a formidable opponent.

"Being an advisor was a stepping stone, right?" he

asked, mostly out of curiosity. "You want to be a politician."

"I never thought I'd simply inherit my father's seat, if that's what you mean."

"I didn't say that."

Further discussion had to wait as boxes and a hand truck arrived. He was amazed by Jana's cool as she gave her friend from security Camille's reason for her exit. Dylan noted she tossed in the university library line for good measure.

The minute they were alone again, he used the interruption to emphasize his point about her career plans. "That's what I mean. The way you connect with people. It's special. Voters like that kind of thing."

"I'll earn it someday. If I represent them with the same amount of concern, I'll keep the job," she replied. "Dad taught me everything I know about acting on behalf of the people, regardless of the issue or party line. It starts with the way you treat the people closest to you."

He let her talk, learning more as he silently filled boxes with books and framed photos, along with a few mementos and awards. She'd mirrored her dad's approach. When someone entered her office, they'd know her credentials, but they'd also see who had inspired her and what issues mattered. Somehow he didn't expect Camille to have the same compassionate, intelligent style.

Once more he wondered about the timing of J.D. Clayton's murder. He'd definitely ruled out suicide after the bikers had shot up Jana's car, assuming it was a political play. But neither of them had pinpointed a policy issue that divided the senator from his closest allies.

Camille had been appointed over Jana. If the senate seat was the goal, no one should bother Jana now. Dylan wondered if he was going after this investigation all wrong. Was the murder personal rather than political? From his study of the family finances, no one was hurting for money or influence. So where was the motive?

Jana's phone beeped with an alarm and she smoothed a hand over her hair, apparently satisfied. Her desk was clear. Each small stack of paper was labeled for her replacement. "That's good enough," she declared. Reaching into her purse, she found her key ring and removed two keys, placing them front and center on her desk.

"So we're out of here?"

She nodded. "By way of my meeting." She added one small box to the top of the stack on the hand truck, then grabbed her purse and a briefcase. "Do you mind hauling this out? I can meet you at the truck."

He shook his head. "Nice try," he teased. "Where's your meeting?"

She gave him the room number that meant nothing helpful about the location. "You can't come with me."

"You're not going alone."

She stood there, the prim and proper expression almost masking the impatience simmering under the surface. But he was learning to see through her. He ignored the urge to muss her up a little, starting with all that silky hair. "Camille won't let either of us back in the building."

She sighed, pressing her fingers to her temples. "Point made. We leave together, but I have to take the meeting privately." She held up a hand, staying his protest. "Not negotiable."

"I'll wait outside the door."

He decided he was losing it when he found her eye roll endearing. Taking control of the hand truck, he followed her through the door. The empty reception room was a lucky break. "Where is everyone?"

"Trailing in the wake of the new senator, documenting her every move. Oh." She stopped and swore quietly, looking around the reception area. "Rose left, too."

Dylan noticed the personal pictures were missing from the desk. "Camille is making friends and enemies already."

Without a reply, Jana hurried to the elevators. When they reached her meeting on the first level of the underground extension, Dylan noticed the room number corresponded with a women's restroom. "Funny," he deadpanned.

"You'd be surprised what gets done where in my world."

He kept his opinion to himself as she went into the ladies room meet her friend.

Dylan used the time to check in with Claudia about the new senator, but nothing helpful was popping up. With so little foot traffic, he left the hand truck outside the restroom and paced toward the rotunda. Reading the directory near the main elevator, he noticed Gregory Atkins's name. Keeping the hand truck and the restroom door in view, he strolled down that direction. Might be interesting to hear Gregory's opinion on the interim senator or even Dylan's scraped knuckles.

Dylan stopped at the sound of raised voices near the office. He peered around the corner, surprised to see Maguire facing off with Atkins. Dylan backed up, taking a seat on one of the benches lining the hall, and pulled out his phone. He wanted to look distracted in case the men came this way or thought to check the security feed later.

He sent another text to Claudia. Gregory and Maguire had been at Camille's swearing in, but no one had told Jana. The reason had to be right under Dylan's nose. He peered around the corner once more, discovering another man had joined Atkins and Maguire. None of them looked happy, but it seemed like Gregory was in the role of whipping boy. Why? Not that Dylan minded.

Jana hadn't reappeared. Dylan sent her a question mark text and she responded almost immediately with a smiley face. Needing to capitalize on the opportunity, he went for the hand truck. He'd walk right by and, if they noticed him at all, he had the perfect excuse to be in this part of the building. Pulling up the camera on his phone, he turned the corner and raised the phone to his ear, faking a conversation. As he passed the office, he held down the button, taking a rapid succession of pictures of the angry trio.

A few spare phrases drifted his way raising the hair

on the back of his neck. "Fired? That makes her sympathetic." That was Gregory.

Maguire's response wasn't clear, but the third man's deep voice was, "What does she know?"

"Nothing," Gregory said. "I told you…"

Dylan couldn't resist, he parked the hand truck just out of view and crept back, straining to catch anything helpful.

"Forget her," Maguire was saying. "Bullet dodged. We have other details to manage."

"She wasn't supposed to be hurt," Gregory said.

"She hasn't been," the third man said. "I've done what I can, but Clayton had others in his pocket, we need to flush them out."

"What about the university guy? There's more to his story."

"He's no librarian," Maguire agreed. "I'll look for any connection to J.D."

"We need to take action," the third man said. "Delays will wreck our chances in the next session."

"Relax." Maguire again. "We can pre-file and this will all be over before anyone else interferes."

It was a rare thing to feel naïve. He knew politicians negotiated, but this sounded far more specific and terribly personal. Dylan's phone vibrated. The text message informed him Jana was done with her meeting. Grabbing the hand truck he replied for her to meet him on the east side of the building.

Outside, he left Jana with the hand truck and rushed for the parking garage, telling himself she'd be safe out here, in sight of the security desk. If the third man had known Jana, chances were she knew him as well. He wasn't sure how to interpret what he'd heard, but it was clear two of the people Clayton had considered friends —Maguire and Gregory—had somehow become the man's enemies. An image popped into his head of Jana taking the oath of office, trusting those who'd helped her get there, and getting cut down in her prime.

While he once again believed the murder was politically motivated, he suddenly wasn't sure that was progress.

CHAPTER 10

JANA WAITED near the hand truck, grateful for the brisk November breeze. Her head was still reeling from the things Tammy told her. Her first instinct was to get somewhere private and tell Dylan, but she'd stepped out of the restroom and he hadn't been there. It had been an immense relief when his text message told her to meet him out here, but given the way he'd raced off, she wanted to know what was going on.

Would Dylan understand the significance of Tammy's information? Camille had already made inroads, clearing a path to pre-file legislation her father had been opposing for years. Jana knew one vote rarely made *all* the difference, but people would expect Camille to represent J.D.'s opinions, especially in these early days. Her father led by example. When he spoke, people listened. Camille could wreck all of that—and hurt Texans in the process—assuming Tammy's information was correct.

A small voice, one that sounded remarkably like a

child even in her head, wanted to scream that Camille wouldn't do anything against her father's wishes, yet here Jana stood, deliberating over proof to the contrary. Unemployed, all of her work effectively seized by an interim senator riding a power high, and her political aspirations derailed for the immediate future.

What was the next step? If she went to the press, she'd quickly be labeled as a bitter and ungrateful stepdaughter. Without access to the office, how were they going to figure out who'd killed her father? Dylan was a good at his work, but he was only one man. While this new side of Camille made her suspicious, other than the weak rumors of depression and marital trouble Jana couldn't see a clear motive for her stepmother to commit murder. As Senator Clayton's wife, she had status and power. In certain circles, she wielded more influence than her husband. They'd been one of the top tier power couples in Texas.

Who was influencing Camille now? Who could possibly be urging her to push through legislation she knew her late husband had opposed?

Spotting Dylan's truck, Jana started that way, thinking maybe her father wasn't the only victim here. He'd warned her things might get ugly. What if Camille was a pawn in a bigger game? What if today's odd behavior was her attempt to keep Jana out of the line of fire?

Dylan's tires squealed as he pulled to a sudden stop. He jumped out of the car, shouting, but Jana couldn't make out his words.

The next thing she knew something hard plowed

into her back. The sidewalk rushed up to meet her and her briefcase was wrenched from her hand. She saw a blur of dark jeans, dark tennis shoes, and a dark hoodie, but couldn't make out any other details.

Dylan ran toward her and she waved him off. "Go! I'm fine!"

She watched, a little awed as his long legs churned in pursuit of the mugger. Her arm stung, her stockings were shredded at the knee and her hip would have another bruise to add to the first.

Jerry, her friend in security, rushed outside to help her up. "Are you hurt, Ms. Clayton?"

"Only my pride." Her favorite heeled boots were scraped worse than her knee, one heel broken completely. Her temper lit like match. "Damn," she muttered. "It took me an entire season to break these in."

Jerry chuckled. "Was there anything sensitive in the briefcase? Do we need to file a report?"

"No. Just the last of my personal things."

"I'm sorry to hear you're struggling. It's expected, of course. Your father was a great man."

"Thank you. Taking care of things for the university library was the last straw for me I guess." She blotted away tears that had nothing to do with sorrow. "I miss him so much."

"I know. I hope someday, when you're feeling better, you'll be back to work here."

"Thank you." She noticed the growing crowd and wished she could just disappear.

"Jana? My word!" Gregory pushed his way through and started fussing over her. "What happened?"

"I was mugged." She had no patience for the way he pawed at her, insisting on helping her walk or how he led her away from Dylan's truck. She stopped short, taking off her boots and going in the direction of her choice.

"You should let them file a report."

"And say what?" Her frayed patience snapped. "A guy in a hoodie stole a high-end leather briefcase. That's it. The pictures inside are probably long gone. He'll hawk it or give it to a girlfriend."

Gregory's mouth fell open. "That's awfully cynical."

"That's fact. I didn't see anything but dark clothing. It happened too fast." Purse on her shoulder, ruined boots in her hand, she boosted herself into the passenger seat of Dylan's truck. She looked past Gregory to smile at Jerry. "Can I just wait here?"

"Of course," Jerry assured her.

"Thank you." She knew they all expected her to dissolve into a weeping puddle of incompetence. While it would lend credence to Camille's decision to let her go, she couldn't quite manage it. Oh, she was overwhelmed, upset to the point where tequila might be more effective than wine, but she refused to have her breakdown in public. Not without Dylan.

She would analyze that small epiphany later.

Gregory hovered though Jerry urged the remaining bystanders away, until finally Dylan loped back into view.

His shirt was damp with sweat, but that was the only

sign of his effort. Her briefcase was clutched firmly in one hand. She wanted to cheer. His sunglasses blocked his eyes, but the smirk on his face gave her the impression he wasn't much more than irritated with the situation. Until he saw her.

His mouth thinned into a grim line. "You're hurt." He stopped in front of her, pushing his sunglasses to the top of his head.

She felt that sharp blue gaze cruise over her body and managed to shake her head. "Not really. You found the briefcase."

"I recovered it." He handed it to her. "The kid got away."

"Doesn't matter." She opened the flap, double checking that everything was still there. "Thank you," she said, gratitude making the words soft.

His hand trapped hers between his hard calluses and the supple leather. "What do you need?"

She didn't understand it, but he steadied her in a way no one else ever had. "A cold beer and a change of clothes," she said, pleased when he smiled. "Then we should probably have a memorial for these boots."

"They were nice." He nudged her into the truck and closed her door.

She watched him exchange a few tense words with Gregory before he got into the driver's seat. "What was that?"

"Communication," he said, his voice gruff.

"Gregory's harmless." They'd been over this last night.

He shifted in his seat, checking the mirrors as they

waited for a traffic light to turn green. "How did your meeting go?"

"Not well." She watched as he checked the mirrors a second time in as many seconds. "You think we're about to be ambushed again." A muscle jumped in his jaw. He wouldn't look at her. "Dylan?"

The light changed and he moved forward carefully. "Can you blame me?"

"You're angry." Since the moment he'd walked into the coffee house, he'd been calm, almost too casual about her situation. Oh, he'd been irritated, with her mostly, and suspicious of everyone, but she'd never seen him like this.

"Not at you," he said.

"That makes two of us, I guess."

He glanced her way before he resumed his assessment of their surroundings. "What happened in your meeting?"

"I'm told Camille plans to support legislation that Dad's been fighting for years."

"Was that legislation at a critical stage when your dad was killed?"

"Not that I'm aware of. Maybe there was something in a committee." It frustrated her that she couldn't be sure. "There were still a few committee meetings on the calendar."

"That you know of."

"Correct," she allowed.

"Who knew about your meeting this afternoon?"

"You and the friend I met with." She resisted the urge to look out the back window at whatever held Dylan's attention. "Unless we missed a bug or they tapped my phone."

"*Uh-huh.*"

He spent more time with his eyes on the rearview mirror than looking through the windshield. It was making her nervous. "Are we being followed?"

"Probably," he said. "But I have a plan. First, what aren't you saying?"

Jana hesitated, pretty sure Dylan wouldn't approve of her alternate theory. "There might be another explanation for Camille's bizarre behavior."

"I'm listening," he prodded.

She braced for a negative reaction. "Everything today was so out of character for her. What if she's trying to protect me?"

He didn't look at her, but she could practically hear him grinding his molars to dust. He made the turn into her neighborhood and drove right up to her house in utter silence. When he'd parked the car and cut the engine he shifted in the seat, tossing his sunglasses onto the dash. "You really can't think badly of anyone can you? It just isn't in you."

"That's not true," she protested. But she lost her voice as he traced the small scrape on her knee through her shredded stockings.

"The mugger?" Dylan asked. "Was he just some misunderstood kid doing his holiday shopping the hard way?"

"You're not funny."

"Good." He pulled the key out of the ignition. "Because I'm not joking. You're in real danger, Jana, and I don't think it stops when you leave the state house."

DYLAN WAITED for her to respond, but it was clear his warning was sinking in. "You know the people around you better than I do. But that makes the reverse just as true."

She bit her lip and he worried tears were inevitable, yet when she faced him her green eyes were clear. "You're saying whoever is behind this knows how to play me."

"They do. Until you change it up."

"I did change it up. I did the unexpected when I hired you."

"That did throw a wrench into the works. Momentarily." Five minutes on the internet would prove he wasn't with the university library. "Which is probably why they bugged your house and office."

"And the mugging was a direct attack?"

"I think so." Another roar of anger sizzled through him, remembering her sprawled across the pavement. "It was well-timed, too."

"I can't think of anything Dad and I both knew that could threaten anyone. He had political opponents, but an enemy with reason to kill him and me? I'm trying Dylan." She sucked in a breath. "I'm trying to see people differently but…"

"Relax." He felt her body trembling through the seat. "Breathe. You're doing fine." He took a deep breath himself, setting the example. "I'll get you through this."

"Okay."

He didn't hear much confidence. "Let's forget it all for tonight."

"What?"

"Banging our heads against it isn't working," he said, relieved when she nodded an agreement. "Believe it or not, I've been fired once or twice. The best cure is a night on the town."

Her hands went to her hair. "You can't be serious."

"It's what normal people do, Jana. They go out, have a few beers, and trash-talk the boss."

"I don't know."

"Trust me," he said. "I'll unload all of this while you get cleaned up, then you can show me the best pool hall in Austin."

"Pool?"

"It's a rebel's game," he teased. "Your future constituents will love you for it. Unless you have a better suggestion?"

She studied him for what felt like a short eternity. "Maybe I do." On that cryptic comment, she hopped out of his truck, gathered her boots, purse, and briefcase and headed for the house.

Dylan grabbed two boxes and followed her. She aimed toward her bedroom and he tried not to think about what she was doing as he unloaded things into her formal dining room.

The house was nice, but it felt like too much for a single woman. Until he remembered the mansion she'd grown up in. Getting back to business, he scanned the house again for any bugs or transmitters. Apparently no one had bothered to wire the house again today.

Hearing the shower turn off in her bathroom, he grabbed fresh clothes and went to clean up. He'd told her to relax and give the issues surrounding her father's death a break, but he couldn't afford to take the same step back from the case. In fact, he wanted to take her out tonight to test a few theories of his own.

Leaving the state house, he was sure they'd been followed right up to the final turn into her neighborhood. Most of her life was an open book, no need to follow her if you knew she was headed home. He was convinced the killer was close to both Jana and her father and he was equally convinced the killer was underestimating Jana's determination.

Tonight could prove interesting, he thought. Dressed in jeans and a casual shirt, he walked out and nearly bumped into Jana in the hallway. Her hair was up in a high ponytail and her deep blue shirt was unbuttoned enough to reveal enticing cleavage behind a lacy camisole. The jeans were practically painted onto her sweet curves and the red heels nearly stopped his heart. He pulled his focus back to her face, noticing the diamonds sparkling at her ears and throat. "I said pool hall," he managed when he found his voice.

"I heard you," she said, sauntering by. "How long until you're ready?"

He was ready now, but not for pool. "Should I change?"

She paused, turning just enough to look him over. It

was all he could do to stand still and take it, when his body screamed at him to take her. Right there against the wall.

A slow smile transformed her face. "You look great."

He escaped into the guest room and tried to breathe. Tugging on his boots, he pocketed his wallet and cell phone and grabbed his keys.

In the truck, she gave him directions east toward the Red River district. "My favorite place has pool, about a thousand kinds of beer, and great bands every night."

"Bands?"

"It's Austin."

"I'm aware," he said before she lectured him further about the music tradition in town. "Do you play pool?"

"Like a shark," she said with a nod. A smile tipped up one corner of her glossy lips.

Dylan scanned the roadway again, disbelief making it hard for him to focus. Or maybe it was the lady seated next to him.

"What do you think happened to our biker buddies the other day?"

Clearly he wasn't being very subtle about keeping watch. "I'm hoping they got picked up by your friend on the Highway Patrol."

"But you're being vigilant."

"It becomes habit in my line of work." He was more than a little relieved when they reached what looked like three bars mashed into one sprawling establishment without incident. He could feel the pounding of a heavy bass beat in the parking lot. "That's a big place."

"I hear getting fired calls for a big night."

He couldn't prevent matching the ornery grin on her face with one of his own. This could be all kinds of fun, especially with someone tailing her. Better if he had an extra set of eyes on their team. Taking out his phone he sent a text message with the address to Swede.

"What are you doing?" she asked.

"Calling in a little backup." He waited for the affirmative response and then pocketed his phone. "Just in case."

"I thought you worked alone."

"Normally, sure." After what he'd overheard and the mugging in broad daylight, he wasn't taking any more chances with her life. If that meant asking for help, so be it.

He escorted her into the wall of sound and the crush of people. Her ponytail swung as she looked left and right before deciding on the best route. She led him past two bars and a stage where two-stepping couples filled the dance floor in front of an energetic band.

Catching his hand, she drew him around another cluster of people and into a long room with pool tables marching the length of the sprawling building. "Call next at a table and I'll grab the beer," she said.

"No." He pulled her to his side, giving the impression they were far more intimate than investigator and client. With a palm on her hip, he reminded her they'd stick together. "We can wait until the waitress comes by."

"That could take a while."

He saw a game wrapping up nearby and took over the table. "I'll survive."

An hour and a half later, after snacking on appetizers and splitting two games of pool, he was convinced watching Jana play pool might kill him. If it wasn't the hips, it was the delectable view when she bent low over the table. Watching her drink straight from a longneck bottle shouldn't be a turn on, but something about it was sexy as hell. He wasn't the only one taking notice, but the admiring cowboys shooting pool around them didn't bug him as much as the guy in the sport coat who strolled by more often than he should. With short, dark hair, he wasn't Patterson's man, Swede. He was only a few degrees below Gregory on the uptight meter. He was also carrying a concealed weapon, but he wasn't part of the bar staff.

Dylan walked up behind Jana as she lined up her next shot, leaning in close to her ear. "Do you know that guy?"

He gave her points for composure. She didn't immediately look, but took her time, chalking the pool cue first. She nudged him back so she could take the shot and when the ball sank into the side pocket, she gave a happy little cheer and a kick of one red high heel.

Strolling around to the table, she lined up another shot and missed. It didn't seem to upset her as she walked over and swiped a French fry off the plate they were sharing. "I've seen him before. That's the man I thought he was following me for several days," she said. "He's why I called you. He was across the street just before we met in the coffee shop. I haven't seen him since, until now."

Dylan absorbed this new information. "You didn't mention this before."

"I thought it sounded paranoid. And I didn't see him after we started working together so I sort of forgot."

Dylan hadn't seen him at all until today. "Reporter or dedicated fan?" he asked, moving toward the pool table.

"I have no idea." She stalled him with a kiss on the cheek.

"What's that for?"

"Luck." She tipped her head toward the table. "You'll need it."

She hadn't left him any kind of clear shot. "I can still take you," he said.

"I'd have to agree." She added a big wink and a Texas-sized smile.

What the hell game was she playing? To an outsider, she might look flirtatious or tipsy, but he knew better. It required more effort than it should to focus on clearing the table and settling the tab.

"Let's dance," she said as they passed by the stage. "My consolation prize."

There were worse places to hide than a crowded dance floor and he could use some time to figure out how to protect Jana and confront the guy tailing her. All thoughts of a threat evaporated as they joined the dancers. Jana's body swayed in time with his and in those heels, her mouth was too accessible. He jerked his eyes away from her rosy lips, up and over her head. He was on a case and she was playing along at his request. Reading too much into her act wouldn't be a smart move. It would be disastrous.

When he tallied up each of the attempts on her life and added in the changing behavior of everyone she'd been close to, he didn't like the result. Political or personal, she was in someone's crosshairs and he wasn't sure he'd figure it out in time. The last time he'd felt this overwhelmed, this incompetent, he'd lost his job.

"We need to talk," he said abruptly.

"Is relaxation time over?" Her hand squeezed the tense muscles in his shoulder. "I was having fun."

"Me too," he admitted, smiling into her lovely green eyes. "The guy we don't know is following us and he's armed."

"Okay." She peered around his shoulder. "So he's probably not a reporter." She licked her lips. "Kiss me."

"What?"

"You heard me." Her fingertips danced along the placket of his shirt. "Come on, Dylan."

He wasn't sure how his feet kept moving when his lips touched hers. The music seemed to fade out, muted by the pounding of his pulse. Pressed against him, he felt her guiding him closer to the edge of the dance floor. "Aren't I supposed to lead?"

"You were leading that kiss well enough," she said. "Follow me."

She guided him down the hall toward the restrooms, passing another couple indulging in a bold, alcohol-induced public display of affection. Braced against the wall, her fingers caught in his belt loops, she pulled his hips to hers. "Is he still there?"

Dylan used the mirror in the corner. "Yeah."

"Tell me when he's gone," she said as her lips met his.

He angled his head, keeping his eyes on the mirror. "Now."

"Hurry." She tugged him into the kitchen and out through the back door.

Together, hands linked, they bolted for his truck. They made it out of the parking lot without any unwanted company, but Dylan knew he wouldn't rest easy tonight unless Swede got more information on the stranger.

Bad enough to learn she was being tailed by an armed professional. The need and desire he felt for her were equally dangerous.

To both of them.

CHAPTER 11

JANA WALKED into her house and let her keys fall onto the table in the foyer. If this was how normal people dealt with getting fired, it wasn't all bad. Of course, she couldn't quite look Dylan in the eye and neither of them had said more than a word or two in the truck. She didn't want to know what he thought of her. Her mind was preoccupied with trying to figure out how she felt about herself.

What had she been thinking with the dancing and kissing? The answer was obvious and she felt her cheeks heat with yet another blush. She wanted to get as close as he'd let her. Well, as a diversion in the moment it had worked. He claimed they hadn't been followed from the club, but then again, she wasn't that hard to find.

She paused at the hallway debating the wisdom of retreating to her bedroom. Better not to let the awkwardness fester, she thought, and headed into the kitchen for a glass of water.

The kisses and her increasing attraction to Dylan had to take a back seat to the reason he was here in the first place. She hit the kitchen light and stared, unable to process the total chaos at first glance. The high of the evening plummeted to an unprecedented low.

Curses poured out of her like a waterfall, but her feet were mired in place, her knees locked as she took in the harsh new reality. Someone had been through her home again. Papers were scattered, both her laptop and his were open on the table, not where they'd been left in the respective bags.

Dylan skidded to a stop behind her and added a few oaths to hers. "You can't stay here tonight." The flash of the camera on his phone shot like bolts of lightning as he documented the damage.

"I'm not leaving." Her voice felt flat, but her stomach pitched and rolled. "Someone was in my house."

He gently turned her away from the mess and into a warm hug. "Let's walk through together," he suggested.

"It's my house." Her legs felt heavy, but it was the prickling of fear skittering just under her skin that kept her moving. "I won't tolerate this."

"Good," Dylan said, taking her hand. "One room at a time."

It was no surprise, but just as offensive to see the boxes from her office had been dumped and examined on the floor of the dining room. "Who does this?"

"Someone desperate," Dylan answered. "I want to know how they got in."

"I have a security system. Don't say it," She held up a

hand, stopping him from pointing out yet again how easily those could be breached. "I should call the police."

He nodded. "Jana Clayton, social policy advisor to the senator would do that."

"Anyone with common sense would do that," she shot back.

He winced. "Walk with me, let me get some pictures before crime scene techs take over."

One hand on her phone, one hand in his, she walked through the rest of the house, cringing at every violation. The den, her bedroom, the bathrooms, not even Dylan's things in the guest room had been spared. "They searched everything but the front room."

"Someone who knows your habits then."

Stating the obvious aloud made her quake. She rubbed her hands over her arms while Dylan sent the pictures to his assistant. "Now can I call the police?"

"In a minute. Who knows your security codes? Who has a key?"

With no sign of a break-in, not even a cracked window, the sensible question bothered her anyway. "Dad and Camille knew the code for the garage. I don't usually lock the door between the garage and the house. I keep a spare key at their house. That's it."

"What about Gregory?"

"He never had a key." She folded her arms across her chest. "Can I call the police?"

"They'll want to know if anything is missing," he said. "Can you answer that yet?"

A scream of frustration built up in her throat, but she swallowed it back. "Impossible to tell from first glance at the papers or computers," she said, ignoring the mess in the kitchen as she stalked down the hall to her bedroom.

Shoving her phone into her back pocket, she poked at the mess, doing a quick inventory of her valuables and jewelry. "All the jewelry is here." Even the ring from Gregory she wished was gone.

"You keep jewelry in interesting places," he said, leaning one broad shoulder against the doorjamb. "Why didn't Gregory have a key?"

She shot him a glare. "What is your fixation with him?"

"That he seems to be fixated on you."

"You realize that makes you sound jealous?" She looked around the room and cringed at the closet. "I really want to clean up."

"Can't do that if you want to call the police," he said.

She felt trapped in her own bedroom with Dylan blocking the door. "I need air."

He stepped aside and she hurried out to the front room and sank into the slipper chair by the window. "Do you think whoever did this got what they needed?"

"Depends on what they need."

"Stop talking in riddles." If she'd call the police, there would be flashing lights, sirens, and help on the way. She laced and unlaced her fingers. "I have to call the police."

"Jana, look at me."

She did. Something about the hard line of his jaw, the serious look in his eyes, settled her down immediately.

"You don't know what's missing, so it's too early to rule out anything. This could be personal. It could be political. It could be about your dad, or it could be staged to discredit you."

"What? Who would believe that? There were plenty of people who can attest that we were at the bar forgetting I got fired."

"And being watched the whole time."

"You think that man was working with whoever did this?" Just when she thought her stomach couldn't twist any tighter, there it went. "Personal," she began, forcing herself to think. "That doesn't fit, despite the clothing scattered all over my room. Nothing's destroyed or broken. Nothing's missing. Random would mean evidence of forced entry and missing valuables."

"Good." He rolled his hand. "Keep going."

"No forced entry might point to Camille, who had access to my house key, but I can't imagine her doing anything like this."

"If you call the police they'll investigate those with access, right?"

"I should hope so."

"An incident like this would make the news and give the public the impression of discord between you and the new senator."

She nodded, reluctantly accepting that possibility.

"Let's say she has an alibi as solid as yours. With nothing missing and no property damage, she could spin it to make you look unbalanced."

She was starting to *feel* unbalanced. "You're right. And Sam made that crack about filling Dad's term being too hard on me." She raised her hands in surrender and tossed her phone onto the coffee table. "What do you suggest?"

"Leave the cops out of it," he said. "We confirm what is or isn't missing and only make a report if we have to. I think it's best if we pretend it didn't happen."

"You said I can't stay here."

He shook his head. "Knee-jerk reaction. No one will get to you while I'm here."

She believed him. "Ignoring it, not reacting, will force whoever did this to escalate again."

There was nothing cavalier or cocky when he dipped his chin affirmatively. "Assuming they haven't found what they're after."

Bottom line, she believed he was the only person who could help her navigate this situation. "So we search it all."

It wasn't how she wanted to spend the rest of the night and maybe those who thought they knew her best would advise against listening to a virtual stranger, but she trusted him. Not just with tonight's mess, but with her life.

DYLAN LET HER LEAD, more than a little relieved she wanted to start with the contents of the boxes strewn about her dining room. The last thing they'd packed, the contents were fresh in their minds. A few of the photo frames were cracked, but nothing seemed to be absent.

He was almost grateful to whoever had broken in.

He wasn't sure what he would've done without the reminder about why he was here. Jana was a client and the sooner he figured out what was going on the better.

His cell phone hummed with an incoming text from Patterson's man. Swede had noticed the same man tracking Dylan and Jana and sent a picture to confirm. Once the tail had lost them, he'd headed out, cruised by Jana's neighborhood and driven back downtown to a mid-priced hotel. Dylan thanked Swede for the report and the assist, but he didn't mention it to Jana yet.

In the kitchen, it seemed both of their computers had locked out multiple attempts to break through the passwords. As much as he griped about it, he had to be grateful for the strict security measures they'd drummed into him at the Guardian Agency. He was also glad he'd kept the flash drives and key in the safe in his truck.

"All the papers are in disarray," she said from where she'd parked herself in the center of the mess. "But it's possible this report on the new safety regulations for transporting oil got some extra attention."

"Was your father for or against it?"

"It was in committee," she said. "We didn't talk about it much." She stacked the loose pages in order. "He was all for safety, but not so much for this approach, though he never told me his precise reasoning."

"Is that the legislation Camille plans to support?"

She looked up at him and he could practically see the wheels turning in her mind. "It's loosely connected."

He waited, but she didn't elaborate. "What did Maguire think?"

He could ask about Gregory, but that would only irritate her. Dylan was not jealous of the man, just concerned about Whiny Greg's loyalties. Particularly after the heated scene he'd witnessed outside the man's office.

"Sam's job is keeping the office running, not promoting legislation or having an opinion."

"If you say so. While you were taking your meeting in the ladies room, I overheard him talking with a couple of other men in an office down the hall."

"That's why you left your post." Her eyes narrowed. "What did you hear?"

She knew that building inside and out and he could tell she suspected which office he was talking about. Knowing he'd get further with evidence she couldn't dispute, he pulled out his phone and selected the best picture. "I meant to ask you about this earlier."

She leaned forward to look and the blood drained from her face. She took the phone and studied the image. For a moment, he thought she was going to throw the thing across the room, but she handed it back with a quaking hand.

"Who's the guy I don't recognize?" he prodded when she sank back against the wall.

"Senator Wayne Price." Her knuckles went white as she dug her fingers into the denim of her jeans. "What could possibly bring Sam, Gregory and Price into the same room?"

"Something personal or political?"

"Neither. Price and my father crossed swords on

every issue. Seriously," she added. "I can't recall a single day that they ever got along. Not one."

And yet two of Clayton's purported friends were right there, chatting up the enemy. "How does Price feel about the safety thing?"

She pushed to her feet. "Oh, you don't need me to spell it out. If Dad was against it, Price was for it."

"Does Camille get along with Price?"

"No!"

Dylan held up his hands. "Ease up, I'm just the messenger."

"What did you hear?"

He cleared his throat. "They didn't use your name, but they mentioned a female who'd just lost her job. Price wanted to know what you knew, but he didn't mention the topic. Sam volunteered to run a background check on me. Giving Gregory credit, he said something about you weren't supposed to be hurt."

She pressed a hand to her belly. "This can't be happening. You said they didn't say my name."

"Did another woman they were connected to get fired today? Would Gregory care about another woman's safety? He was right there, dancing attendance after the mugging." Dylan wished he'd chosen a different phrase. The thought of dancing only brought the sensual heat of holding her close to the front of his mind.

"It doesn't make sense. Gregory and Sam have been loyal to Dad since forever."

He understood what she was going through.

Betrayal like this cut deep. "I have a question and you aren't going to like it."

"Oh, yay." She leaned against the counter, her eyes steady as she waited.

"Is it possible your dad shot himself because of the people and problems stacking up against him?"

"You're right, I don't like that question." She shoved the papers back into boxes and stormed off down the hall.

He felt like an ass, but he'd been there himself. When he didn't hear a door slam, he walked down the hall, stopping in her doorway. "Every man has a limit. If his wife and best friend turned against him—"

"He would've had me!" Her voice broke on the last word and she clutched a flat box over her heart. "We've always had each other."

Dylan clenched his fists. He wanted to hold her. It was remarkable how much he wanted to ease her pain, but touching her was too risky. "Up until a few years ago I wore a sheriff deputy's badge in Montana. You see the dregs of humanity when you're working law enforcement."

She slid him a look, then returned the box to the top drawer of her dresser. He wondered about it, and stopped wondering as she gathered bits of silk and lace, dumping it all into the laundry hamper.

"But you meet good people, too. A woman I'd met on a case asked me out long after the case was closed. We went out and things got serious. I started thinking about diamond rings and how to proposal. Where we'd live, how many kids we've have, and all the rest."

Jana stared at him and he forced himself to go on. "What I'd thought was love turned out to be a blinding lie. It didn't matter that she fooled everyone right along with me. I was closest to her, *I* should've seen through it. When she betrayed *me*, when it all came out, costing me my job and my reputation, I took a hard look at my gun cabinet."

"Dylan."

"I'm just saying I've been there, Jana." He took a step into the room and when he wanted to reach for her, he forced his attention to the clothing scattered at his feet. He scooped up the garments and carried them to the hamper. "It messes with your head learning someone close to you is capable of that kind of deception and that you couldn't see it. As if that wasn't bad enough, before I had a chance to prove my innocence, my father suffered a heart attack and died. Now he'll never know it was her and not me."

"Oh my God, Dylan, I'm so sorry."

He grabbed another wad of clothes and headed for the hamper.

"But you didn't kill yourself."

"No. I'll never work in law enforcement again. It's not easy to accept that, it's even harder to know I can't make it right with my old man. So I ran away, ashamed and disgraced."

"You left your mom and sister… and friends?"

He nodded. Not his proudest moment and he'd just dumped it out there, hoping his old pain would somehow ease her grief. "Headed for Mexico, I got stalled out in San Antonio because of a barroom brawl."

"But you're here now."

"Yeah." He still didn't know how he'd been found. "An attorney showed up and offered to spring me if I signed on to this job."

"Do you like the job?"

"Some cases are easier than others." Each case had challenges, but Jana's was turning into an emotional trial. He didn't dwell on his past, preferring to keep it buried since he'd found renewed purpose with the Guardian Agency. He checked on his mom and sister weekly. He'd even gone home for Christmas last year. "It doesn't erase my mistakes, but it's good work."

"Do you go back to Montana?"

"Occasionally." They were getting off track, but seeing her relax was worth it. "My mom's been making noise about seeing me again for the holidays this year."

"You should go," Jana insisted.

He nodded. "Maybe."

Jana worked in silence for a few minutes, picking up and restoring order. The holidays were going to be rough for her, especially if this new facet of Camille was the real thing and not an act to shelter Jana from something worse. He had serious doubts about that theory.

"My dad didn't kill himself," she said suddenly, her voice soft. "If he sensed the betrayals, he would've taken action."

"Action which got him killed."

"Yes, but..." The scowl lifted from her face and he watched a new determination spark in her eyes. "If he thought it would come back on me, he would've done something. Or tried to."

"You're thinking about the letter."

"He did tell me I shouldn't trust anyone."

Dylan hooked his thumbs into his back pockets. "Trust is overrated," he agreed, but she wasn't listening.

"Just my intuition."

He remembered that line and as she held his gaze he had a sinking feeling about the next conclusion she was leaping toward. "Jana."

"Where's the hate mail?"

"The hollowed out book is in my truck, but I sent images to Claudia for review."

Jana urged him out of her room, toward the guest room. "They tossed the house looking for the hate mail." She hurried across the hall and stared at the much smaller mess in his room. "Whoever did this didn't even try to make it look like a real search in here." She spun around to face him. "It is someone who knows me."

She seemed so happy about it he didn't dare burst her bubble with another dire warning. He wouldn't let anyone get past him to harm her, but he needed to know what was on her mind. "Can you do a little of that thinking out loud?"

She was practically dancing as she slipped by him, heading for the kitchen. "Check in with Claudia while I take a look at the email I skimmed from Dad's account today."

He did as she asked, pleased to finally see full background history going back to Camille's college days. Grades, jobs, connections, milestones, the woman had a way of sticking close to people with power, influence, and money. He turned his computer to share the report with Jana.

"Your assistant is good. There are some things here I didn't know." She squinted at his screen and pointed at one item from a few years back. "Can you please ask her to check the legal stuff behind that corporation?"

Legal stuff? She sounded as weary as he felt. "Sure. Will it shed any light on your progress with your dad's email?"

"There are time gaps in his official account. It's like someone went in and deleted certain items." She rubbed her eyes.

"You need some rest," he said, pulling his laptop out of her reach. "We can pick this up in the morning."

"I'll make coffee," she said. "We should take a closer look at his private account."

He managed to block her path to the coffee pot. "You can't be planning a sneak attack on the state house?"

"His study would be better."

"Oh, it'll be so much easier to go unnoticed there."

She covered her heart with her hands and heaved a dramatic sigh. "With no job, where else would a daughter struggling with her grief go?"

Having seen her in action he believed she could sell it just that way. She'd been convincing enough when she kissed him nearly brainless earlier tonight. "We'll talk about it in the morning." He laid his hands on her shoulders, intending to turn her around and aim her at her bedroom, but she slid her hands across his chest.

"Thank you, Dylan."

His entire body came to full alert, ready and eager

for more of her caresses. He had to restore some professional distance here. "For what?"

"Sticking with me. This can't be easy on you." She brushed her lips across his. "Good night."

He stared after her, wondering how she managed to keep him off balance. He wanted a cold shower. Correction, he wanted Jana more with every minute, but this wasn't the right time. Thinking of her as a client wasn't nearly the effective deterrent it should've been. He'd once been accused of having a weakness for witnesses. It was a load of crap, but the claim still haunted him.

There was one big difference between the situation in Montana and the situation here. Jana wasn't a fraud.

CHAPTER 12

Over breakfast the next morning, they took the time to go through both flash drives, coming up empty again. Jana knew her father had written that letter—*by hand*—because he suspected the worst. He'd wanted to avoid an electronic trail. It was up to her to figure this out and protect his legacy. What on earth was she missing?

She refilled her coffee cup, catching a teaser that the new senator would be on the local morning show in an upcoming segment. "Sam's been busy." She hoped the words didn't sound as bitter as they tasted on her tongue. "Camille will be out of the house."

"What about the housekeeper?"

"She'll be at church. After that sometimes she goes to see family." Thinking of Helen's loyalty to Camille made her cringe. "There's no way to know when she'll leave or how long she'll be gone. Between the two of us we should be able to manage her as long as Camille is out.

This could be our best chance for another look at the study."

Jana was surprised when Dylan didn't argue. In fact, he ushered her to his truck before she'd finished her coffee. During the drive to the Clayton ranch he'd filled her in on the added details he'd received from Claudia about Camille's connections with the one company who stood to gain the most if the oil transport safety legislation passed. Jana was stunned. Could the woman she had considered her second mother for more than a decade really be this conniving?

When they found the estate empty, Jana gave a weary cheer. She encouraged Dylan to park behind the house so they could enter the study through the courtyard with her father's master code.

"Does Camille know you can do that?"

"Probably not. I figured out the master codes when I was in high school."

"You snuck out of the house." The look he gave her was pure admiration. "So it wasn't always stargazing that pulled you out into the dark."

"No comment." She'd never connected her minor teen rebellion with her more circumspect solution as an adult. Somewhere along the way she'd purposefully hidden her real self from her closest friends and even herself, apparently, determined to make her dad proud. It baffled her and she wasn't sure how to shift her habits, how to take a chance with a new relationship and how to be just Jana Clayton.

Glancing around the study, she pulled herself back

to the more urgent matter at hand. "Where should we start?"

"Who cares?" He grinned at her. "I want to hear about you being a rebel."

She laughed. "Not today."

"I'm only teasing." Dylan dropped his hat on the nearest chair. "See what you can do with his email. I'll see if there's a lock hiding around here that fits this key." He turned on the television, keeping the volume low, waiting for Camille's interview segment to air on the morning show.

She spent several frustrating minutes searching through her dad's personal email. He'd forwarded a few of her analyses and some suggestions from Sam. None of it related to the questionable legislation or any of his concerns within his committees.

"There has to be something." She signed out of the email account and started searching through his cloud storage. There were photo albums, letters of thanks or encouragement, news stories that had inspired or concerned him, but nothing that made her sit up and take notice. "What have we got?" she murmured, sitting back. "A key, a secret stash of hate mail, and a personal letter."

"Don't forget odd alliances," Dylan added, showing her a framed picture of Camille and Sam flanking her father. The smiles were as bright as the sunshine flooding an outdoor stage.

"His last campaign." She smiled as the memory resurfaced. "He decided to go old school," she said. "Talking issues and taxes in as many small venues as possible. The way he and mom did it during his first campaign." She looked over the shelves for that picture and didn't see it. As she surveyed the shelves again and again a distant memory surfaced, taking her back twenty years. "Where did you say you found the key?"

Dylan pointed to the small statue on the bookshelf. "In the base of the same statue in the state house office. But this statue isn't so helpful."

"Sweet Jesus." She knelt in front of the cabinet under the shelves. "It couldn't be…" She opened the two doors of the cabinet and reached inside, moving her hand over the shelves inside.

"What're you thinking?" Dylan knelt beside her.

"Mom bought him the first statue when he won his first campaign. She bought him the second one to keep at the office when she found out how sick she was. She told him that no matter where he was, at home or at the office, he would always know that he was her star." Jana smiled as her fingers found what they were looking for. She popped the face off of a custom drawer hidden inside the cabinet. "I can't believe it."

"What is this?"

"I used to play in here all the time when I was little. One day, I was probably nine or ten, I tripped it by accident. I thought for sure I'd found a treasure chest."

"You're a little scary."

The approval in his voice almost made the ordeal worthwhile. Almost. They only had as much time as Helen decided to spend with her family after church. While they had practiced their explanation and exit strategy, it would be better if they didn't get caught in here at all. She had to hurry.

"My father must've had the remodelers build the new bookshelves and cabinets just like the old ones."

Jana pulled out the long metal box that had been hidden by the drawer front and set it on the desk. "It's a old bank lockbox."

"From a Texas bank that closed decades ago," Dylan said as he fished the key out of his pocket and handed it to her.

Jana didn't ask how he could know that as she accepted the key. Her hand was steady as she fit it into the lock. With a quiet 'pop' the latch gave.

More papers were topped with three DVDs. They were labeled with dates, except for one, labeled FYI in block letters. She exchanged a look with Dylan before she slid the first one into the drive on the computer.

Within a few minutes it was clear the video documented meetings between her father and his allies here in the study. She picked up the one that wasn't dated, noticing it was a different DVD brand from the others.

A couple in formal wear come into view, lips locked and hands pawing at clothing. Jana blushed, belatedly recognizing the dress as she reached out to stop the playback. "Oh my God. That's Camille."

"It's the study," Dylan said, "but that's not the same angle as the other videos." He was moving around the room, looking for cameras when the man's face became clear.

"Oh." Jana clapped a hand over her mouth and

turned away, not sure if she could avoid vomiting if she continued to look.

"What? What's wrong?" Dylan turned back to the monitor and started laughing. "Go Whiny Greg. Did you know he could do that?"

"That's awful." She waved a hand at him. "Make it stop."

A moment later the only sound in the room was Camille's voice on the television. It did nothing to make Jana feel better.

"There's no date on this," Dylan said.

"It happened over Memorial Day," Jana said. "The dress. I recognize it." It was all the explanation she could manage.

"Unless things have been rearranged, it was filmed from over here," Dylan said. "But your dad's camera is up there." He pointed to one of the upper bookshelves.

"Why would she do that? Everyone thought they had a great marriage."

"You don't sound as angry as Whiny Greg's potential wife should be."

"I told you I never planned to say yes. Gregory is a fool, but she… I can only imagine how Dad felt when he saw this." She rubbed at the headache building behind her eyes. "He must have been hurt and furious. Camille wouldn't have left him. Not for Gregory."

"You're right," Dylan agreed, "he's too small a fish for her."

It sounded downright mercenary, but Jana was starting to agree with Dylan about Camille's true nature under the layers of savvy businesswoman, devoted wife, and kind stepmother. "Then what could Gregory have that she wanted?"

"Besides the obvious?"

Jana ignored the jab, rethinking the past session, the votes, and when her father had started keeping things to himself. The safety legislation hadn't made it to a senate vote, but a new rail yard had been fiercely debated.

"Claudia can dig up anything within hours," Dylan offered.

"It's worth a look. I don't feel like I know anything about these people anymore." She ejected the DVD and pointed to the television. "The interview is wrapping up." She didn't know what she wanted, beyond some clear answers. Turning off the computer, she took the papers from the secret drawer and stuffed them into her purse along with the offensive DVD. Putting everything to rights, she heard the security system signal someone coming through the gate.

Dylan checked the monitor. "Looks like Maguire's car."

"She must have refused a live interview, forcing the station to prerecord it. We have to hurry," Jana said. "This way." Leaving the study, she led him back toward the part of the house only family was allowed to enjoy.

They sank into a big leather sofa as she turned on the television and switched it to the morning program. She reached for a tissue from the box on the end table just as a door chime sounded. Voices, a man and woman, started in the kitchen and came closer and she recognized Camille's flirty tones talking right over Sam's deeper voice.

Jana shifted closer to Dylan and laid her hand on his firm thigh. Clearly understanding what she was after, he draped an arm over her shoulders, making the scene look much more intimate than it was.

Camille stopped short. "This is unexpected." She looked to Sam who only raised his eyebrows.

Jana pretended to swallow back tears. "I miss him so much." She waved a hand around the room. "I needed to be close."

Camille's expression softened. "Bless your heart." She crossed the room settled on the ottoman in front of the couch. "I made you handle everything, not seeing the toll until it was almost too late." Rubbing Jana's knee with a perfectly manicured hand, she turned to Sam. "Can you please bring in some tea? Mr. Parker can help you."

DYLAN FELT Jana's body tense up, but she didn't need to worry. He had no intention of leaving her alone with Camille. "We can't stay for tea," he said. "I think Jana's had enough this morning."

"She needs family right now."

"Oh, he's right," Jana argued. "I couldn't possibly keep you from your new responsibilities and I do have an appointment." She gave a quiet sniffle and then lifted her watery gaze to Maguire who hovered at the other side of the room, clearly uncertain how he should proceed. "You and Sam must have an enormous list of things to cover."

Camille's heavy perfume clogged Dylan's nose. Either he'd lost his instincts as an investigator or these two had been taking some personal time while the rest of Texas thought they were in the studio.

Camille had used Gregory for a currently unknown reason and had ensured her husband knew about it. Had she done the same thing with her husband's best friend and confidant? Dylan and Jana had been looking for an outside catalyst determined to get the senator to cooperate on some vote or issue.

Dylan now understood that it was far more personal, more intimate, than that.

Jana put on a brave face as Camille insisted on discussing the interview. Dylan kept a mental scoreboard of the veiled compliments from Jana and the increasingly edgy replies out of Camille. The woman didn't want Jana anywhere near her new political arena, that was crystal clear.

That was fine by him. Jana was in real danger. They needed to get out of this house and possibly out of Austin if they were going to properly evaluate the threat before someone took aim at her again.

Maguire walked over and tapped his cheek just under his eye. "You walk into a bookshelf or something, Parker?"

That's right, Dylan thought, *take a jab at me for a change.* He rubbed slow circles across Jana's shoulder, silently urging her to let him take the lead. "Is it showing already?" He tapped his face, just under the bruise. "The mugger caught me off guard," he said.

"Mugger?" Camille looked to Jana, then Dylan. "Who was foolish enough to target you?"

The hungry, hunting gleam in her eyes made his skin scrawl.

"I was the target," Jana said in a small voice. "Dylan chased him down for me and saved my laptop in the process."

When the color drained from Camille's face, Dylan wanted to lean over and kiss Jana for playing this so perfectly.

"Crime is becoming such a problem for Austin. We should beef up that part of the platform, Sam," Camille urged, making a nice recovery.

"Sure," Maguire replied automatically. "When did this happen?" His gaze was locked on Jana. "Did you report it?"

Camille pushed to her feet. "That's it. I can't have you two rushing away. Jana, come with me while I make the tea. Your friend can explain. I don't want you reliving what must've been a terrible ordeal."

"You're right," Dylan agreed. "She's been through too much already."

"I'm fine," Jana assured Camille. She aimed a wobbly smile at Dylan. "Dylan is taking the best care of me."

"That's something positive," Maguire muttered.

"I think so." Standing, Dylan helped Jana to her feet, keeping her hand in his. As he reached for his hat, he caught the silent exchange between Camille and Maguire. "We need to get going." He handed Jana her purse. "You'd be surprised what we have going on today.

We're already behind. You don't want to be late," he said to Jana.

Jana nodded, lowering her face and dabbing at tears. "I shouldn't have taken the time to come here, but it really helped me think things through."

"I'm glad." Dylan pressed a gentle kiss to the top of her head. He couldn't wait to see how Camille and Maguire reacted to that.

Jana reached out to hug Camille, but didn't let go of his hand. "I hope you don't feel I intruded."

"This is your home, too, dear."

"I can call someone," Maguire blurted. "It wouldn't take long to file a police report."

Dylan settled his hat on his head. "No thanks. There's nothing to report since the kid got away. Unless you think there's something on the security cameras."

"What cameras?" Maguire glanced at Camille. "You added security cameras to the system at your house?"

"Oh, no. I was mugged at the state house," Jana explained. "Jerry was so helpful. He can tell you all about it." She looked up to Dylan. "We really should go. I don't want to be late to my appointment with Jen."

"Wait!" Camille gasped. "I heard about that incident, but I didn't realize it was you. Why didn't you call me?"

Standing so close, Dylan felt Jana shiver. He'd bet his entire commission the cause wasn't fear, or sorrow, but suppressed anger. He squeezed her hand for moral support.

"On the day you were sworn in?" Jana shook her head. "No, I couldn't ruin that for you," she said with convincing sincerity. "Dylan was there. He's been such a rock for me since Dad di-died," she finished with another delicate sniffle.

This time, Dylan excused them effectively, breathing a sigh of relief when they were finally on what he considered the safe side of the Clayton estate gates. "That was interesting. Did you see his face when I mentioned the cameras?"

"Yes." Her voice was hard, her temper clear. "And Sam smelled like he'd rolled around in Camille's perfume."

"Are you surprised?"

"No," she admitted.

"You held it together, Jana. You did a great job."

"You were worried she'd get in my head if you left me alone with her."

He laughed. "I don't trust her, but I had other reasons."

When she faced him her eyes were wide. "Which are?"

"Her safety and my paycheck. I can't protect you if you get locked up for assault."

"Aw, you're so thoughtful." Her burst of laughter filled the cab. "Prison-orange probably wouldn't be my best color."

He thought she'd look hot in just about anything. Further proof he needed to stay on point and wrap this up quickly. "Who's Jen?"

She laughed again and this time it had an edge to it. "I'm sure Camille and Sam are trying to figure that out right now. There are three likely options."

Dylan slid a glance her way. This would be good.

"There's Jen who's in charge of the annual Junior League holiday fundraiser," she said, holding up one finger. "Then you have Jen, the governor's wife, or maybe I'm planning to meet the Jen who is my counterpart in Senator Price's office."

"Well played," he said with admiration.

"Thanks. But now what? Should we take the DVD to the police?"

"Are they into homemade porn?"

"Ewww." She smacked him on the arm. "Seriously. Would that be enough to reopen an investigation into the cause of dad's death?"

"You hired an investigator," he pointed out. "Me."

"True, but—"

He cut her off. "Did the police listen to you before?"

"No."

"Did the woman in the sex tape just fire you?"

She sighed and slumped back into the seat. "Yes. And if I turn over the DVD I look like the petty stepdaughter."

"You said it."

"Then I guess it's back to my place to go through the things we found in Dad's secret box."

"Maybe." He switched lanes, watching a dark sedan move with them. Damn it. Camille had to be in it with Maguire, for something more than the sex and the obvious support for the senator's seat. There'd been too much silent communication between them. "Which Jen do you think will freak them out the most?"

"Why?"

"We're being followed."

"Again?" She swore. "You practically told them we were going back to my house."

"I know." He glanced over and gave her a smile. "Which Jen?"

"The governor's wife. Her mom and mine were close and she has all kinds of connections. If I was looking for a sympathetic ear or in need of help politically or personally, she would have the most influence."

"Why didn't you take your concerns to her?"

"Rather than your agency?"

He nodded, moving again to keep the driver tailing them on his toes.

"Like I said when we met, I needed someone who could look at the situation objectively."

"Right." He might've met that definition when he came to town, but he didn't feel so objective now. Jana mattered to him beyond his professional obligation to her as a client. It wasn't exactly smart, but denial wouldn't make anything better. He was sure as hell attracted to her, the chemistry was obvious. But when he looked at her he sensed something deeper, something foreign and uncomfortable.

Potential.

He didn't do well with potential. His or anyone else's. He could protect her and he'd be more than happy to take her to bed, if she chose to go slumming with a guy like him. Anything more than that—anything personal or emotional—felt like standing at the edge of a cliff with a knife at his back. Jump or take the blade, both solutions made him the loser.

"What are you thinking?"

He glanced in his rearview mirror again. "When people point guns at you they're on motorcycles. This guy is following us, but not shooting."

"Can't we be happy about that?"

"We could." But he was thinking of the report Claudia had provided on Camille. Between the corporate connections, her proven infidelity, and her audacious confidence, it wasn't a stretch to paint her as the brains behind the senator's murder. "Let's try something different." He changed lanes again and headed across town to his hotel.

"There's a drawer under your seat," he told Jana. "Put the things from your dad's office in there. I can lock it with the key fob."

"Do I want to know what you're thinking?"

"Probably not, but I'm not risking another mugging." He made the next turn and watched as the sedan did the same thing. "If this is the same guy from last night I want to hear what he has to say, but I want to hear it on neutral ground."

She nodded, turning to get a look. "Then what?"

He shot her a quick wink. "That depends on what he says."

This time they pulled through the driveway and parked near the back entrance of his hotel. He locked the safe and the truck and escorted her straight to his room. "When he shows up, I want you to hide in the bathroom until I tell you it's safe."

"No."

"Jana, I know how to do my job."

"I'm aware of that."

Someone knocked on the door. Damn. He didn't even have time to text Swede. "Go." He ignored her irritable look as she marched into the bathroom.

Dylan pulled the gun from his holster and checked the peephole. "Who is it?"

The man, the same guy from the bar, held up a badge and identification from the Texas Rangers. "Just need a few minutes of your time, Mr. Parker."

Now we're making progress, Dylan thought, opening the door. "Come on in."

CHAPTER 13

JANA GAVE up her efforts to calm the butterflies swirling and dive-bombing in her stomach. They'd been at it for hours, since the moment her life had undergone another gravitational shift when Texas Ranger Victor Ramirez entered Dylan's hotel room. Ramirez was the man she'd thought had been following her. For good reason, because he had been.

Life shouldn't be this complicated.

Maybe life wasn't, but murder sure as hell was.

It had been gratifying to have her suspicions confirmed and to hear her father had been taking the steps to protect himself from dangerous political and personal threats. His enemies had simply moved more quickly than expected. Even talking it through, looking at the hate mail her father had forwarded to Ramirez, the staged suicide didn't fit the anticipated timeline.

Dylan and Ramirez assured her an unpredictable criminal made more mistakes. She'd have to take their word on it. At least now, after combining all of the information they'd narrowed the suspect pool to two: Camille and Sam. Both had access to the study, and both stood to gain significant power and money if the new legislation for safety protocols regarding oil transport were passed.

Now, with Ramirez working in the background, she and Dylan had to create an opportunity for either Camille or Sam to make a mistake or to confess. Her stomach pitched and the butterflies did barrel rolls to compensate. She wasn't sure how she was going to pull this off. Dylan promised her he'd help her through it. Following her dad's advice, she trusted her intuition about both Dylan and Ramirez. Which was good since they were putting things in motion tonight.

Holding her breath, she willed her hand to remain steady as she applied eyeliner and mascara. She'd never worn so much makeup—not even on Halloween—but that was the point. No one was supposed to recognize her or her behavior while they were out tonight.

Jana pulled the hot rollers from her hair and bent at the waist, giving her head a shake. She stood up, a bit startled by the volume of thick glossy curls tumbling around her face. Her hair tickled her bare shoulders when she moved her head. Maybe the racy halter top was too much. Maybe the clingy red skirt was too short. Maybe none of it mattered. The look was completely different from the conservative, tailored wardrobe she donned every day.

"Mission accomplished," she whispered to her reflection. "Let's go."

Leaving her cell phone behind as he'd asked, she

tucked fifty dollars into her bra and forced herself to walk out of her bedroom.

Dylan waited in the kitchen, absorbed with whatever was on his laptop screen.

"Will this work?"

His head came up slowly and she knew she'd hit the mark with the disguise when Dylan's eyes went wide and his chin dropped. He'd called her stunning when she'd dressed for dinner with Gregory, but this time she didn't know what to expect. "Too much?"

He shook his head. "Perfect."

She should've known he wouldn't mind her slightly trashy fashion statement. He rarely aimed judgment of any kind her way. But when he looked at her like that she wanted to dress this way every day. Well, at least every night. More specifically, she wanted to forget the plan and drag him to the nearest horizontal surface. If only she had the courage to venture further than those hot kisses. Her intuition told her that sex with Dylan would be life-changing, but that it would also take more than she was ready to give.

"I don't think we should play pool tonight," he said.

"It's the skirt, right?" She tugged at the hem. "I can change."

"Don't you dare." He stood, but hesitated on his side of the table. "When you were a rebel, where did you go?"

She felt her cheeks heating. "We'd go dancing at some rough honky tonks outside of town."

"I knew you had a wild side under all that restraint and polish."

"Is that supposed to be a compliment?"

"Oh, yeah." He stepped closer, wrapping a curl of her hair around his finger. "Why didn't anyone ever tell you good girls are allowed to cut loose?" He bent his head and kissed her lightly. "We'll find the right mix of work and play, I promise."

She trembled, believing him completely. Whatever soap or cologne he wore made her think of long kisses in dark corners. The man tempted her like no one else. "What were you working on?"

"Research."

"Do you have something more on Camille?" If they didn't have to go out they could stay in. She didn't know which would be worse—or better.

"No." He edged past her toward the foyer. "I was looking up Austin nightclubs."

"I could've told you about that."

He took her shawl from her arm and draped it across her shoulders. "Maybe I wanted an objective opinion."

What was he up to? "You're sure this is the best option?" She didn't like leaving her house exposed overnight.

He just smiled and opened the door. "The sooner we go, the sooner it's over."

And the sooner he'd be out of her life, she added, feeling frustrated. That wasn't at all what she should be thinking about. They had to navigate this part of the plan to expose her father's killer. As she walked to his truck it took all her willpower not to look around for whoever was watching her house. This was an essential risk. One designed to bring this whole scheme to a head. Only the people watching her and Dylan would know the house was empty, or where to find them.

In the truck, Dylan turned up the music and she tried to relax enough to get in the mood for bar hopping. "You think they'll come after me again tonight?"

"Ramirez is making sure the right people hear about our chat with him this afternoon."

Unless they were wrong about Camille and Sam, but she couldn't quite make herself believe that anymore. "I know we need to be sober, but I'm having a huckleberry margarita at the first opportunity."

"No problem." He reached out to touch her hair again. "Any chance tequila makes your clothes fall off?"

"Stop it," she said, when she realized that was the song playing on his radio. "I was being serious."

"So was I."

His deep voice sent another shiver through her and she couldn't pull enough words together to make a coherent sentence. Sometimes silence was better.

"Here's to old times," Dylan said, pulling into a parking space in front of a club designed to look like an old, battered saloon. Bouncers checked ID's at the door while the band on stage had the crowd on their feet.

Honoring her request, Dylan guided her straight to the bar, the palm of his hand on her back. When he had his beer and she had her huckleberry margarita, they found just enough room to stand and enjoy the drinks. She drank hers too fast, but she needed the liquid courage to play her part.

"I don't like knowing they're watching me." Her gaze darted around the club, but she couldn't spot anyone taking an interest in them. Yet.

"Forget them. It's my job anyway. And if you see a big blond man with a wicked scar on his face, don't worry. He's with us."

"The backup you called in?"

"Yes. He's from Montana too, though we'd never met before this. He works for a company called Brotherhood Protectors. Former SEAL, all around badass, and on our side," he assured her.

She spotted the man he'd described. There couldn't possibly be more than one man like that in all of Texas. "Far wall," she said. "Do you think fish in a bowl get nervous when people stare?"

Dylan chuckled and traced her jaw with his finger. "Swede isn't the staring type." He raised her chin, giving her a long study. "Did you like knowing *I* was watching you those first nights?"

Suddenly her body remembered the feel of him on top of her when he'd pinned her down in her backyard. A shiver slid through her system and her knees threatened to buckle. Wouldn't it be wonderful when Dylan caught her? "I didn't know you were watching me."

"But now you do."

The husky timber of his voice heated her blood. His eyes, that impossibly blue gaze, had her wishing he'd look at her with that intensity forever. "We need to dance." It was the only way she could get her hands on him and not go too far. And it was the only way to tempt her father's killer to make a move. On her house, or on her, but either way she and Dylan had to make this look real.

He led her out to the dance floor and the music pulsed around them, through them, drawing them close until her heart seemed to beat in time with the bass, while her body moved sinuously with Dylan's. His hands brushed her hips, her shoulders, her bare back, even the sliver of her midriff left bare between her top and the skirt.

"Check the phone," he said, as he brought her close after a turn.

She lifted his phone from his shirt pocket. "Ramirez. Two men just went into my house."

He bent his face close and his lips brushed against her ear. "Hang on baby, it's about to get interesting."

"Someone's here?"

"Eyes on me," Dylan said, when her gaze leaped across the dance floor again. "I've got this." A few minutes before the alert, Dylan had spotted the welcome wagon team he'd fought with the night she'd had dinner with Whiny Greg. It was possible the pair was connected to the killer, but after their talk with Ramirez, Dylan felt more confident that the would-be fiancé had hired the thugs to rough him up.

Caught between a jealous man and a political power play. Not the ideal elements of a date. Which he supposed was fair, since this was a job. "Have you ever thought of taking a vacation and getting out of town?"

"Who doesn't?" Her eyes were full of determination. "But we can't run off when Ramirez is counting on us tomorrow."

He'd analyze her use of 'we' and 'us' later. "Oh, we'll be there." Despite what the clowns in the corner had in mind. Given a chance he'd happily pound these two into the dusty parking lot for interrupting his dance.

Whether it was the tequila, the music, or feeling anonymous, Jana had finally relaxed. When he'd told her she looked perfect, he'd meant it. Not for an evening in a honky tonk, not for the game of cat and mouse, simply perfect. Hair up or down, in jeans or a suit, the woman was in his blood. Unfortunately, he could already tell she'd stay there long after the case was closed and he left town. He admired her grit, her ethics, and her instincts.

Jana's eyes went wide as someone tapped firmly on his shoulder.

"May I cut in?" the man asked.

Dylan turned, facing the Silent Partner from the other night. "So you *can* talk." He punched him in the throat. "Answer's no," he added as the man staggered back and fell into another couple.

If Dylan understood anything about human nature, it was how to stir up a bar fight. No matter where you were from, it rarely took much to piss off a drinking man. Talker came up behind Jana and grabbed her around the waist. "We'll take her home for you."

"Go on and try that. I dare you," Dylan said. From the corner of his eye, he saw Swede approaching and signaled him to hang back.

"Dylan!" Jana shouted and kicked as Talker backed away, but she didn't have a good angle to do any real damage. "Dylan!"

He dogged Talker's every step, his eyes on his target. The dancers made space for a fight, but the band played on as the bouncers closed in. He didn't have much time and he might not have another opportunity. "Get your hands off her."

Talker pulled a knife, pressed it to her neck. "Your night's over, hot shot."

"Oh, I don't think so." The blade stopped everything. *Everything but Dylan*. He took another step forward as the hush fell across the room. "Last chance."

The bouncers were clearing the floor and probably calling the cops. Swede had positioned himself where he could help if necessary. It wouldn't be necessary.

"How much did Atkins promise you?" Dylan asked.

Talker sneered. "Enough."

Dylan smiled. If Atkins was involved, these two had orders not to hurt Jana. "I hope so." Dylan took another step. "Assault with a deadly weapon in front of all these witnesses." He shook his head. "Probably not your first offense either."

"Back off."

"No." Dylan saw a bouncer moving taking up a post opposite Swede and behind Talker, but he wanted a piece of this bastard first. He grabbed a beer bottle from the nearest table and threw it at Talker's head, on the knife-hand side.

The man blocked the bottle and Jana stomped on his foot, scrambling away as Dylan charged in, throwing upper cuts. It wasn't a fair fight, even before the knife fell from Talker's hand. An upper cut, a right cross, and a knee strike and the man was mush on the dance floor.

The crowd burst into applause and Jana rushed into his arms. For a moment, he just held her. "You okay, sweetheart?"

Her cheek rubbed against his shirt as she nodded.

"Good." Dylan turned to the bouncer. "You can take him from here?"

"Happy to," the big guy said. "Any chance you teach classes?"

"Not tonight," Dylan shook his hand. "Sorry for the mess." He glanced over to see Swede melting back into the crowd.

"This is nothing compared to the usual," the bouncer said. "You pressing charges?"

Dylan wrapped an arm around Jana. "That's up to her."

She shook her head.

"Guess not."

Jana wrote a number down on a bar napkin and handed it to the bouncer. "Call this number to cover any damages."

Dylan waited until they were outside to ask her about the note. "Did you give them Atkins's number?"

"At the office," she said. "He'll never be able to dodge that call or the responsibility."

"You're brilliant." Dylan gave her a squeeze.

"I have my moments," she agreed, leaning into him. "What now?"

He opened the truck door for her, then went around

to the driver's side. "Another club?" he asked, starting the engine.

"I don't think so."

Dylan's phone hummed, and he was checking the update when the rear window shattered. "Get down." Slamming the truck into gear, he pulled out of the space, kicking up dust and aiming for the highway. After a minute or two, when it didn't seem like anyone was on their tail, he let her settle back into the seat. "It's safe."

"What was that?"

"An attempt on your life. At least to scare you to death. If you can find my phone, let Ramirez know Atkins was behind an attempted kidnapping back there."

She groaned. "Gregory wouldn't have known where we were unless..." She groaned again rather than complete the thought.

"He has to be in on it," Dylan finished for her. "You must be his prize for cooperating."

"But why take a shot at me?"

"Because whoever killed your dad is more worried about what you know than Gregory's feelings or ability to retaliate if he's cheated of his prize. Tell Ramirez we're done for the night."

"Good."

"He'll understand that to play our part tomorrow we need to lay low tonight."

She plucked at her skirt. "I can't face off against Camille and Sam looking like this."

"You won't have to. I packed a few things while you were in the shower."

"You did what?"

"I packed a few of the basics." At least from his perspective. He slid a glance her way. "Don't worry, it'll go with those boots."

She laughed softly. "You're a sucker for these boots."

"I'm a sucker for all of you," he said before he could stop himself. "You've really held up."

"You didn't expect me to."

"No," he confessed. "I didn't expect any of this." There. He'd been honest with her, even if he didn't specify what he meant by 'this'.

Considering the options and their timetable, he decided against a cheap motel. She deserved better after all the craziness. He'd use an alternate ID and credit card so Camille and Maguire couldn't trace the transaction and he had a spare plate for the truck in the tool kit though he couldn't hide the wrecked window.

Life was about chances, he thought, backing into a parking space camouflaged by shrubbery in the parking lot of one of the most elegant places in town. He booked a room from his phone and then took care of the license plates while she waited in the cab. After taping a sheet of plastic across the back window and sending an update to Swede, he opened her door. "I'm ready."

She just looked at him for a long moment. "Guess this isn't the first time you've had this kind of trouble."

"Probably won't be the last time." He grinned as he unlocked the safe under her seat. Shooting her a wink, he reached between her legs. "Time to finish our homework."

Gathering up everything important from the truck, he led her into the lobby. When they were settled in the room, she started pacing. "Do I need to get you a drink?" he asked.

"Water's fine."

"Do I need to listen?" He sank down on the king sized bed and watched her, waiting.

She shook her head and stared through the window over the sparkling Austin skyline. "You called me baby when we danced."

And sweetheart after a thug had held a knife to her throat. "That offended you?"

She turned, scooping her hair back from her face. "No." She seemed a little surprised by the admission. Crossing the room, she held out her hands. "Let's finish that dance."

"Jana." He resisted when she tried to tug him to his feet. This couldn't end well.

"I need to feel something other than grief or betrayal, Dylan."

"You heard Ramirez. We're almost done. Then you'll be safe and free to feel anything you want." He tipped his head toward the desk. "What about the homework?"

"Not tonight. We can wake up early in the morning." She leaned in close, her body brushing lightly against his as she swayed. "Please, Dylan."

Where was an interruption when he needed one? "I'm not the man you need." Though he damn well wanted to be. He was too jaded for her, too rough to fit into her gleaming, polished life.

"You're the man I need right now." She pressed her soft lips to his jaw.

He went hard in an instant. One night. *Right now*. It was exactly how he did things. He smoothed his hands over the swell of her hips, knowing he should step back. Walk away. She wanted to be a politician and being with him would drag her down.

He couldn't do this. Even just one night with him, knowing the scope of his past failures, could ruin her dreams. Worse, it scraped him raw that he wanted more than right here and now. He'd vowed never to leave himself that vulnerable again.

"It's adrenaline," he told her. "It'll pass."

She reached down, cupping his erection and stroking him through his jeans. "Will it? Feels like you have an adrenaline rush going, too."

He closed his eyes. A seduction? Out of the prim Ms. Clayton? "You're playing with fire," he warned, knowing his control could snap any second and leave her singed.

Her eyes were sparkled when she looked up at him. "I know. I'm burning up." She licked her lips as her fingers dipped behind his belt.

He pushed his hand into her hair and covered those full, luscious lips with his. She tasted sweet and so, so hot. Pleasure scorched him from the inside out and he gave up thinking about anything beyond this moment in this room.

He untied the knot of her halter top, letting it fall away. The pale skin of her breasts swelled against the sleek satin cups of her strapless bra. He cupped her breasts, his thumbs teasing her nipples to hard peaks as he backed her toward the bed.

She fell with a laugh onto the soft mattress and he followed her down, pinning her hands over her head. He wanted to feast and discover and indulge in every inch of her. If she kept up this pace, it would be over too soon.

She flexed her hips. "This is better than the backyard," she murmured between kisses along his throat.

"Careful with those knees tonight," he replied.

In answer, she wriggled one leg free and wrapped it around his.

Shifting, he dipped a hand under her skirt, relishing the toned muscles and soft skin. Exploring more, he found the high hem of her panties riding the curve of her bottom. "Ms. Clayton, you surprise me."

Her smile promised all sorts of wild delights, but her voice was soft. "Let me touch you."

He kissed her, long and deep, until they were breathing for each other. Releasing her, he pushed back to his feet. He saw the protest on her rosy lips die as he yanked off his shirt and tossed it aside.

"Very nice." Her gaze locked on his bare chest.

He put his hands on his belt, but stopped. "You're falling behind." Would she play?

Her eyes gleamed with a wicked light and she sat up, tossing her hair over her shoulder as she unhooked her bra.

He sat down long enough to remove his boots. "Leave those on," he said when she reached for hers.

There was a dangerous fantasy in his head and if he could only have one night with her he wanted to make the most of it.

Standing, he worked his belt loose, then undid his fly and pushed off his jeans.

She took her sweet time looking him over before she came to her feet. Her grin was sharp and her breasts thrust forward as she lowered the zipper at the back of her skirt. It pooled on the floor and she stepped out of it, closer to him.

"Seems I'm still overdressed," she whispered.

"My God." She was a vision, a thousand times more beautiful than he deserved in her black satin panties, red hot boots, and all that gorgeous hair spilling over her shoulders.

"Back at ya." Her voice was a rasp against his senses and she ran her hands, then her lips over his chest.

He kissed her mouth, trailing open-mouthed kisses across her skin in a sensual discovery of shoulders, breasts and belly. On his knees in front of her he removed that last scrap of fabric and teased her with lips, tongue, and fingers until she was gasping and quaking on a climax.

With his name echoing in the air, he caught her and fell to the bed. Her hair spread in waves across the pillows and her legs wrapped around his hips as he drove into her hot, slick core.

Need clawed at him, building with every thrust into her welcoming body, until she clutched with another climax, carrying him along with her.

Spent, he nuzzled her neck, before reluctantly

rolling to his side. Whatever time he had left with her, he wouldn't regret it.

But he wouldn't waste time labeling the experience with passionate words and impossible promises either. He might want more—from himself and her—but it couldn't work. Wouldn't be fair. She was destined for a great public career, and his business skirted the fringes of the law, not to mention the disgraceful end to his first career. Her enemies would use her association with him against her and he couldn't bear to cause her any harm.

She meant too much to him.

CHAPTER 14

JANA SAT up and dispensed with the boots, surprised at how easily she'd embraced his sexy game. She hadn't ever had *fun* in bed with her short list of sexual partners. "And men say they don't care about fashion," she teased, tucking herself next to Dylan's strong, lean body. It would be a miracle if she ever learned to breathe normally again.

"You should let that side of you out more often," he said on a quiet laugh.

"I'll make a note."

"Not tonight." He shifted, pulling her on top of him and wrapping his arms around her. "Tonight you stay right here."

She felt... cherished. Love was too strong a word and way too soon, though she suspected she could fall for him. He was different and it had nothing to do with geography, his lack of an accent, or her upbringing.

Politics was always a thorny road, and you had to have tough skin and adaptability to get through, but she'd never anticipated the brutal betrayals that ended her father's life. Did she really want to be part of that unpredictable and slippery system going forward? Her father had done good work, cultivated a spirit of honor and duty in her heart, but maybe there was a better route for her. The clouds of this conspiracy would be hard to chase away even if they managed to coax the confession Ramirez wanted from those involved.

Dylan brushed a fingertip across her brow. "You're frowning. Want to talk about it?"

"No." She levered up and over him, turning out the light. "I have better things to do." Under her hands, her lips, his hard body came to life once more as she slowly explored him with all the attention he'd devoted to her.

MONDAY, *November 19*

Hours later, as the first wisps of sunlight filtered through the sheer curtains, she came awake under Dylan's soft kisses and enticing touch. It was an indescribably marvelous start to what would hopefully be her last dangerous day for a long time. She opened for him, body and soul, knowing that if things went right, he'd soon be gone from her life. It didn't seem fair, but what could she do? She refused to give herself any reason for regrets.

They ordered room service and pored over the papers her father had hidden and she still didn't have the answers she needed—about the case or Dylan.

Ramirez had the men who'd accessed her house in

custody, but they weren't revealing any connection to Camille or Maguire. Which left Senator Price. "I know Ramirez wants us to connect Senator Price to the murder, but I don't see it," she said.

"He met with Atkins and Maguire."

She groaned. The reminder wasn't necessary.

"You don't have to solve this alone." Dylan smoothed her hair back over her ear.

She hadn't pinned it up yet. After last night, she might wear it down all the time. Though it could prove counterproductive to have a constant reminder of her time with Dylan. "Show me the hate mail," she said.

He pulled it up and turned the laptop so she could scroll through at her own pace.

"What if Senator Price is the patsy?"

"How do you figure? You said he didn't have access to the study."

"Not for the murder. That had to be Sam or Camille." She congratulated herself for saying the words without tossing up her breakfast. "But for the politics. The vote in the next session. What if he's being led along just like I was?"

"I thought he wanted the new safety legislation?"

"It won't profit him nearly as much as it does Sam. Of the three of them, only Sam needs the money. Camille just needs to hang on to what she inherited from Dad's estate. She's after the power."

Dylan nodded, but he didn't look convinced. "Walk me through your thought-process."

"These two phrases sound like Sam. I've been listening to him spin bad news into good all my life," she said. She shuffled the papers until she found what she was after. "But here," she pointed to the screen, then to the page. "This is a direct *inversion* of my analysis." She opened a window showing the original document.

"I'll be damned."

"It must be what tipped off Dad."

"So your father hid the paperwork and wrote that letter to warn you after he alerted Ramirez," Dylan concluded. "Now we just have to figure out who pulled the trigger."

She sat back, pressing her hands to her eyes. "And what Sam's got on Senator Price." She sighed. "I never thought I'd be helping that bastard."

"What's Price most interested in?"

"Himself. His primary business is cattle," she replied.

"He'd have access to rough men willing to earn a little cash the hard way?"

"Of course." Jana couldn't believe she hadn't thought of it before. "Still, what leverage are they using against him?"

"I'll have Claudia take a closer look, but it could be as simple as capitalizing on his hatred of your dad."

True enough. If anyone could convince a person to see things in a new light, it was Sam. She couldn't understand what had pushed him to such a low point that he'd kill a lifelong friend, but she wasn't sure she wanted to. It seemed like her father and Ramirez had been banking on the friendship and her dad had paid the ultimate price. Then again, if Camille pulled the trigger…

Dylan's cell phone rang, putting an end to the

disturbing speculation. If things went right, they'd have a confession soon and this would all be behind her.

She watched him pace to the window and back. When this wrapped up Dylan would move on to the next case and the next person who needed his protection. She tried to be happy about it, for him and his future client, and couldn't quite get there.

"Ramirez is ready for us to move."

"The house is empty?"

Dylan nodded.

"He wired the study?"

"That too," he said, dropping into the chair next to her. "You can do this, Jana. I'll be right there beside you. I will keep you safe."

She nodded, then reached out and kissed him. "Promise me something."

He smiled. "Whatever I can deliver is yours."

"When this is over, I want one more night with you."

DYLAN SMILED. "IT'S A DEAL." He loved the way her mind worked. Loved *her*.

The realization astonished him and while he wouldn't lie to himself, it wasn't something he could say aloud. He didn't dare. Not because of his past, though associating with him would plague her political aspirations. No, telling her meant the inevitable, polite reaction would haunt every day of his future. How else could she react? They're differences went deeper than profession and geography. She might be into him now, but her career required a husband who didn't run off on assignment every other week.

He'd made the most of the moment, he thought, swallowing the last of his coffee. He'd had Jana in those sexy boots, first thing this morning and again in the shower. Too bad for him, he wasn't close to satisfying his craving.

He called himself an idiot for feeling anything at all. Examining the paperwork demonstrated how different they were. Nothing as simple as background or geography, they were light years apart socially and possibly further than that morally. She was all about good work and while he thought of himself as a good guy most of the time, he worked in some shady areas. Looking at every layer he'd peeled back on this case only proved he'd do more harm than good if he told her about the nonsense clattering around in his head.

He was a bodyguard and an investigator and as soon as she wasn't in danger, the agency would move him to another case.

She wanted one more night with him. He tried not to get his hopes up. If they got the confession for Ramirez, he vowed he'd tell her every ugly fact about Montana and give her the chance to walk away before she gave him so much as one more sweet kiss.

It was the least he could do. She made him want to do and say things he'd never dreamed of after leaving Montana.

On the drive to the Clayton ranch he reached across the cab and caught her hand. "Relax. It will be fine."

"They killed my father." No pain in her voice now,

only steely determination. "You may have to keep me from clawing her eyes out."

"I'm a bodyguard. You can count on me to do whatever is necessary to guard your best interests."

"Thanks."

CHAPTER 15

THEY WAITED in her father's study for a reaction to the bait Ramirez had created. With any luck, the next few minutes would supply answers to the questions that had plagued Jana since they'd found her father dead of a single gunshot wound to the head. She wanted to know why, despite Dylan's warning that the answer would most likely disappoint her.

"Helen?" Camille's cultured voice rang through the house. "Helen?"

"Told you we should've changed the locks," Dylan said. "Then we could get her on breaking and entering when she came through this door." He jerked a thumb toward the door that gave anyone with the code direct access to Senator Clayton's study.

Jana braced for the worst, reminding herself how good it would feel when the house was hers again. "Would've tipped our hand," she murmured as the sound of Camille's heels clicked across the slate floor.

As Camille rushed through the open study doors,

Jana stood up from her father's chair and raised a pistol. Sam was right behind her stepmother, an inconvenient twist, but certainly nothing Jana couldn't adapt to.

"Stay right there," Jana said, leveling the barrel at Camille. Her stepmother stopped short and a mean sort of irritation twisted her typically serene features. "Dylan told me what you did," Jana continued, "how you treated my father. I've sent the evidence to the news networks," she said, sticking with Ramirez's script. "Within an hour, the rest of the world will know, too."

Sam swore. "Put that down, honey. Let's talk it out." He stood shoulder to shoulder with Camille, the solidarity painfully obvious.

The good-old-boy condescension ticked her off. "We're way past that, Sam. Nothing you can say will make this right."

"Honestly!" Camille barked. "What in the world are you talking about? You can't possibly put the lies of this man," she flung an arm toward Dylan, "over your own family. I won't allow the Clayton name to be dragged through that kind of mud."

"Better if I wallow in the mud you've been flinging around?" Jana took a breath, willed herself to slow down and do this right. "You've spread lies about my father being depressed and marital trouble. Dylan has been a thousand times more honest with me than either of you."

"Please." Camille crossed her arms over her chest and raked Dylan head to toe with an appreciative gaze. Jana wanted to punch her. "Woman to woman," Camille said, "I'm sure he was good in bed, but that's as far as this can go. Your father wanted better for you and I can make sure the right things happen for you professionally and personally. You can keep him on the side if you must." She slid another hungry look toward Dylan. "But he's a predator. Did he tell you he lost his job in Montana because he slept with a witness to coerce a statement? Did he mention the San Antonio jail cell?"

Jana almost laughed at the absurd accusations. So what if he'd made mistakes? Dylan might be a lot of things, but unethical wasn't one of them. "I know all I need to know about him. Dylan didn't kill my father. *You* did."

"This man has fed on your grief and filled your head with nonsense," Camille said, her voice softening to something resembling pity. "You're smarter than this."

Jana played along, hoping she managed to look baffled rather than eager. Dylan did his part, his vivid blue gaze steady as a laser. She knew emotions made him twitchy and this wasn't the time for him to crack, but she hoped someday he'd trust her enough to share a smidge of his feelings.

"Your father's suicide didn't make this easy on any of us," Sam added.

"Stop!" The statement yanked her attention unmercifully back to the immediate issue. "I know you killed him," she said. "No matter which of you fired the gun, you're both guilty." She hated the quiver in her voice as she said it, but at least her gun hand was steady.

"This has gone on long enough," Camille snapped, stepping forward. "You're old enough to think for yourself, Jana. You've been played by a two-bit con artist."

"Says the woman who slept with a man half her age. A man I was seeing." Jana delivered the line as if Gregory mattered. She just had to hold out, extend this horrible awkwardness a few more minutes. The video was running, she could see the tiny red light glowing on the bookshelf.

"What?" Sam looked to Camille. "What does she mean?"

Jana turned her attention to Sam. "You didn't know about Camille and Gregory? I'll forward you the video."

Jealousy might make him give up information the police could use against Camille. The longer this went on, the more Jana considered that doing time for double homicide would be worth it. She dragged herself back from that slippery slope of vengeance and stayed with the plan. Dylan, his backup man, and Ramirez had her covered no matter what Camille and Sam tried to pull.

"What did she promise you, Sam? Tell me you didn't sell out Dad for sex."

Sam's gaze slid from her to Dylan and back again. He shook his head. "You've got this all wrong."

"Enlighten me." She aimed the gun right at his heart.

Sam started babbling. "Your Dad was out of touch. He didn't understand how quickly things were changing in the real world."

"Then we failed him," Jana said. "It was our job to give him the information to make the right choices. The choices that would better the lives of his constituents."

Camille snorted. "Your father's ideals were outdated. Old fashioned," she admonished. "I'll be sure the right legislation goes through as it should just as quickly as possible."

Incredulous, Jana lowered the gun slightly. "You killed him over the new oil transport regulations?"

"If he changed the vote I promised to the investors and contributors, we were all dead anyway," Sam admitted. "Your father had powerful enemies."

"My father had character and integrity which is more than I can say for either of you."

"Put the gun down," Sam said. "Be reasonable before this becomes a career-ending situation for you."

On a brittle laugh, Jana lowered the weapon, following the plan. She even sank into her father's chair, setting the gun on the desk, but keeping the barrel pointed at the pair of murderous liars in front of her. "What career? Camille ended that when she fired me."

"I gave you a leave of absence because you're grieving." Her stepmother's voice dripped sharp, hurtful blades. "Your father did wonderful things for the state of Texas, but it's time for new direction. Everyone will be happy to see you in a few months, when you've recovered and are an asset to my campaign."

Again, Jana wanted to shoot. She wanted to leave them with wounds and scars that cut as deep as their betrayal of her father. "You've got it all planned out and the second payoff spent, don't you?"

Camille gave Sam a long look. "Spent?"

"Oh, did Sam keep a secret from you?" Jana taunted. "How defiant of him."

For a blissful moment, Jana and Dylan were forgotten while Camille aimed her venom and fury at

Sam. They bickered about sex and money, about votes and plans, until finally Sam spilled the name of the company who'd paid him a bonus when he'd promised the senator's vote and support.

It was all Jana could do to keep her eyes away from the video camera. As if he sensed her distress, Dylan gave her shoulder a squeeze.

She thought of the agony Sam had put her father through with the threatening letters and breathed a little easier knowing Sam would serve hard time for all of it. But which one of them had performed the ultimate betrayal? She clamped her lips shut, thinking of the pain and heartbreak her dad must have endured in his final breath.

"Shut up about Gregory!" Camille shrieked. Her palm connected with Sam's cheek in a loud crack and he staggered back. "An ally in the prosecutor's office was essential to the plan."

Jana's stomach twisted, much as it had when she saw the video the first time. Gregory was hip-deep in this mess, too.

"You didn't have to sleep with him," Sam barked.

"And you said you wouldn't have to kill J.D.," Camille retorted.

"I didn't!" Sam shouted it, his eyes whipping to Jana. "She did it. She shot your—"

"Liar!" Camille screeched.

Startled, Jana was a second too slow. Camille grabbed the gun from the desk and fired at Sam. Thank God Dylan had loaded the weapon with blanks.

"He did it," Camille said, lowering the gun. "J.D. told

him he couldn't support the new regulations and Sam killed him."

"No! She did it," Sam protested. He sputtered, coughing from the impact while he patted his shirt as if waiting for the blood to appear. "Blanks?"

"Yes." Jana said, relieved as the wail of emergency sirens surrounded the house. "Care to add anything else? As an old friend of the family," she said.

"Your dad was like a brother to me."

Jana nodded. That's what made the entire situation incomprehensible. "I know."

Camille pointed a shaking finger at Sam. "He set the whole thing up." Tears tracked down her face. "He made the deals. He said the letters would be enough to keep J.D. in line."

Jana didn't believe either one of them and was more than happy to let the Texas Rangers take over from here and sort things out. As Camille and Sam were cuffed and hauled away, Dylan took down the video cameras while Jana handed over the material they'd found.

She peered through the blinds, spotting the news crew Dylan had contacted. "Thank you," she said.

"You're welcome."

"I'd probably be dead by now without you." She certainly wouldn't have been any closer to the truth. "I can't believe how blind I've been." She pressed her hand to her belly. "Downright naïve. Camille was right about that. I won't make that mistake again."

~

WHEN JANA FACED HIM, Dylan saw the hesitation, the damned *doubt* in her gorgeous eyes. It was a good thing Maguire and Camille were in custody. He wanted to tear them apart with his bare hands. She wasn't thinking about her dad or politics now, she was thinking about the next step. About him.

Earlier she'd asked for one more night. Would she renege? He should've told her the whole truth, should never have held back any part of the fiasco that drove him out of Montana. Whatever she decided, he deserved.

He had a momentary reprieve as Swede walked into the study. "You all set here? I'd like to get back home."

Dylan laughed and introduced Jana. She thanked him and the former SEAL's hard edges seemed to soften. "No one should have to deal with a mess like this. Glad I could help."

"Me too," she replied. "If there's anything you need, please don't hesitate to call."

Swede arched a pale eyebrow. "Good to know. Thanks. My wife, Allie, has talked about taking a Texas vacation." He tucked his hands into his pockets. "I'd never seen the appeal, but you've got some great nightlife."

Dylan shook hands with Swede and walked him out. "I really do appreciate Hank sending you down."

"Want some advice?" Swede offered.

Dylan shrugged. "Sure."

"Don't let her go, man. She's a keeper."

"I know."

He just wasn't sure he was the sort of man Jana

wanted to keep around. Best to lay it all out and let her choose. He walked back into the study and found her pacing. "Jana, I need to tell you—"

"Stop." She held up a hand. "You don't owe me any explanations."

"What Camille said... about the coercion... that case wasn't like that."

"Of course it wasn't," she replied, sitting back into her father's chair.

He stared, sure he'd heard her incorrectly. "How do you figure?"

"I know you better than that." Her lips curved, the smile wobbling at one corner. "Camille's a crocodile. I wouldn't take her word about a weather report."

"You deserve the truth."

"Dylan, stop." She shook her head this time. "Your past isn't my business."

Her insistence threw him off. He'd been ready to confess and braced for the rejection.

Could she possibly be as nervous as he was about parting ways? Technically, her case was closed. He'd done his job and she was safe now. Once Claudia had his final report, he was free to leave Austin and Jana Clayton behind. Yet, he couldn't bear the idea of never seeing her again. "What about my future? Is that your business?"

"I'm not sure," she said quietly. "I suppose that depends on your plans."

Obviously she was going to make him say it. All of it. "I'd like my future to be your business." He wasn't sure how to make her understand just how much he wanted to stay in her life. Not for the sex, though their chemistry in bed would be reason enough to carry this out a few months.

Her lips twitched as she studied him. "Are you asking if I want to stay involved with you?"

He pushed a hand through his hair. He was making a mess of this. "No. I want more than that," he clarified as the hope drained from her expression. He took her hands in his and pulled her out of the chair. "Years ago a woman used me. She told me what I wanted to hear, gave me what I thought I needed and it and cost me everything. My career, my reputation, even my family. I was too ashamed to stick around and hope they'd forgive me."

"You—"

He kissed her hard and fast. "You've only heard part of it. Just listen."

She stared up at him, her eyes gleaming, but not with tears.

"I've only told one woman other than my mother and my sister that I loved her. She didn't deserve those words and I swore I'd never trust another woman enough to say them again." He kissed her when she started to interrupt him. "Life has a way of humbling me and I can be a pretty slow learner, but I can't leave Austin until you know the truth. I love you, Jana Clayton. Like it or not, you're the only person who can help me figure out what to do about it."

"Really?" Her eyes danced with something akin to mischief.

He grabbed her hips and brought her up against him. "Which part isn't clear?"

"All of it," she said, running her fingertip across his lower lip. "Say it again."

"Once is all you get until you say it back."

Mock indignation on her face, she poked him in the shoulder, but didn't wriggle out of his embrace. Instead, she wound her arms around his neck and brought her mouth close to his.

"I love you, Dylan Parker."

The words brushed softly over his lips and the kiss that followed was sweeter than a huckleberry margarita.

"Good," he growled, stopping just long enough to catch his breath. His heart raced with the possibilities. *She loved him.* Whatever happened, he wouldn't have to try and forget her. "Think it through. For you, I'll stay behind the scenes and dream with you in the starlight, but my history is no asset to your career."

"You'd be amazed what a good chief of staff can spin. I hear politics can be a dangerous game. If I pursue that route, I might need a bodyguard. Of the permanent variety."

"I know a guy." He shrugged. "Or two."

She laughed, kissing him until they were both breathless.

He leaned back, brushing his lips against her hair. "What do we do about it? About us?"

"In the short term or long term?"

"All of the above," he replied, resting his forehead on hers.

"In the short term let's do this." She kissed him again, her mouth hot and full of tempting promises.

"Reasonable," he rasped.

"I thought so." She nipped at his jaw. "Long term?" She forced her face into a dubious attempt at a somber expression. "You should know what you're getting into."

"Do tell." He started backing her out of the study, into the hallway.

"I'm currently unemployed. I have two houses and an obscene amount of money, not counting what I'll get when Camille's trust is returned to the estate."

"That could be a major court battle." It would take time for the legalities as well as the trauma to pass. She'd want to redecorate and rebuild her family home into a place she could enjoy without sorrow. He guided her toward the den where she'd told him she enjoyed so many happy childhood memories with her dad and mom.

"I'll win."

"It will take time," he teased.

She cocked her head. "I just said I was wealthy enough without it."

"As if I love you for your money." He ran kisses up and down her neck. "Maybe we should just plan on putting anything recovered from Camille the crocodile into a trust for the kids."

"Kids?" Her smile was blinding. "As in our kids?"

"Jana, sometimes when a man and woman love each other—"

She smacked him playfully on the arm.

"If you don't want kids, that's fine," he said. "It's no hardship to keep you all to myself."

"I want kids," she blurted.

"With a guy like me? You better be sure. The only property I own is a decent truck, I'm not sure about my employment status, but I have a healthy bank account."

"How healthy?" she teased.

He pushed her back over the arm of a leather sofa and followed her down as she laughed. "You already said the words, before you knew the numbers," he reminded her.

Her eyes went soft. "And I meant those words. I love you, Dylan, with all of my heart."

He saw the truth of it in her eyes and knew she could see the same thing when she looked at him. "You're mine."

"Forever," she agreed, sliding her hand to his nape and bringing his mouth to hers once more.

The kiss, making love to her right here, would be the first of countless new, happy moments they would create. Together.

ABOUT THE AUTHOR

Regan Black, a USA Today and internationally bestselling author, writes award-winning, action-packed romances featuring kick-butt heroines and the sexy heroes who fall in love with them. Raised in the Midwest and California, she and her husband enjoy an empty-nest life in the South Carolina Lowcountry where the rich blend of legend, romance, and history fuels her imagination.

For book news and special offers, subscribe to Regan's newsletter.

Keep up with Regan online:
www.ReganBlack.com
Follow Regan on Amazon
Follow Regan on BookBub
Facebook Reader Group

BROTHERHOOD PROTECTORS WORLD

ORIGINAL SERIES BY ELLE JAMES

Brotherhood Protectors Hawaii World

Team Koa Alpha

Lane Unleashed - Regan Black

Harlan Unleashed - Stacey Wilk

Raider Unleashed - Lori Matthews

Waylen Unleashed - Jen Talty

Kian Unleashed - Kris Norris

Brotherhood Protectors Yellowstone World

Team Wolf

Guarding Harper - - Desiree Holt

Guarding Hannah - Delilah Devlin

Guarding Eris - Reina Torres

Guarding Payton - Jen Talty

Guarding Leah - Regan Black

Team Eagle

Booker's Mission - Kris Norris

Hunter's Mission - Kendall Talbot

Gunn's Mission - Delilah Devlin

Xavier's Mission - Lori Matthews

Wyatt's Mission - Jen Talty

Corbin's Mission - Jen Talty

Tyson's Mission - Delilah Devlin

Knox's Mission - Barb Han

Colton's Mission - Kendall Talbot

Walker's Mission - Kris Norris

Brotherhood Protectors Colorado World

Team Watchdog

Mason's Watch - Jen Talty

Asher's Watch - Leanne Tyler

Cruz's Watch - Stacey Wilk

Kent's Watch- Deanna L. Rowley

Ryder's Watch- Kris Norris

Team Raptor

Darius' Promise - Jen Talty

Simon's Promise - Leanne Tyler

Nash's Promise - Stacey Wilk

Spencer's Promise - Deanna L. Rowley

Logan's Promise - Kris Norris

Team Falco

Fighting for Esme - Jen Talty

Fighting for Charli - Leanne Tyler

Fighting for Tessa - Stacey Wilk

Fighting for Kora - Deanna L. Rowley

Fighting for Fiona - Kris Norris

Athena Project

Beck's Six - Desiree Holt

Victoria's Six - Delilah Devlin

Cygny's Six - Reina Torres

Fay's Six - Jen Talty

Melody's Six - Regan Black

Team Trojan

Defending Sophie - Desiree Holt

Defending Evangeline - Delilah Devlin

Defending Casey - Reina Torres

Defending Sparrow - Jen Talty

Defending Avery - Regan Black

BROTHERHOOD PROTECTORS
ORIGINAL SERIES BY ELLE JAMES

Beau (#4)

Rafael (#5)

Valentin (#6)

Landry (#7)

Simon (#8)

Maurice (#9)

Jacques (#10)

Brotherhood Protectors Yellowstone

Saving Kyla (#1)

Saving Chelsea (#2)

Saving Amanda (#3)

Saving Liliana (#4)

Saving Breely (#5)

Saving Savvie (#6)

Saving Jenna (#7)

Saving Peyton (#8)

Saving Londyn (#9)

Brotherhood Protectors Colorado

SEAL Salvation (#1)

Rocky Mountain Rescue (#2)

Ranger Redemption (#3)

Tactical Takeover (#4)

Colorado Conspiracy (#5)

Rocky Mountain Madness (#6)

Free Fall (#7)

ABOUT ELLE JAMES

ELLE JAMES also writing as MYLA JACKSON is a *New York Times* and *USA Today* Bestselling author of books including cowboys, intrigues and paranormal adventures that keep her readers on the edges of their seats. When she's not at her computer, she's traveling, snow skiing, boating, or riding her ATV, dreaming up new stories. Learn more about Elle James at www.elle-james.com

Website | Facebook | Twitter | GoodReads | Newsletter | BookBub | Amazon

Or visit her alter ego Myla Jackson at mylajackson.com
Website | Facebook | Twitter | Newsletter

Follow Me!
www.ellejames.com
ellejamesauthor@gmail.com